Reader's Digest

BEST LOVED BOOKS
FOR YOUNG READERS

The Jungle Books

A CONDENSATION OF A BOOK BY

Rudyard Kipling

Illustrated by Paul Jouve

CHOICE PUBLISHING, INC.
New York

The illustrations are reproduced from wood

engravings by Paul Jouve for *Le Livre de la Jungle*,

published in 1919 by the Société du Livre Contemporain,

in a limited edition of 125 copies.

The black-and-white decorations were drawn by

Rudyard Kipling's father, J. Lockwood Kipling, for the

first editions of *The Jungle Books*, published by

Macmillan, London, in 1894 and 1895.

PRODUCED IN ASSOCIATION WITH MEDIA PROJECTS INCORPORATED

Executive Editor, Carter Smith
Managing Editor, Jeanette Mall
Project Editor, Jacqueline Ogburn
Associate Editor, Charles Wills
Contributing Editors, Elizabeth Prince and Melinda Corey
Art Director, Bernard Schleifer

Library of Congress Catalog Number: 88-63377
ISBN: 0-945260-26-1

This 1989 edition is published and distributed by Choice Publishing, Inc.,
Great Neck, NY 11021, with permission of The Reader's Digest Association, Inc.

Manufactured in the United States of America.

10 9 8 7 6 5 4 3 2

OTHER TITLES IN THE

Reader's Digest

BEST LOVED BOOKS
FOR YOUNG READERS
SERIES

Foreword

THESE VIVID AND dramatic stories of nature, and of the man-child adopted by jungle beasts, have become part of the basic treasure of English literature. Here are Mowgli, the wolf-boy, and his protector, the black panther, Bagheera, and his formidable enemy, Shere Khan, the lame tiger. Here is the gallant story of little Rikki-tikki-tavi, the mongoose who took on Nag, the cobra, the scourge of the jungle; and here, too, are Toomai, the elephant boy, and the White Seal who had a vision, and Purun Bhagat, the wise man who spoke only with animals until the last, when he spoke to humans with mighty effect. All these tales cast a unique spell, a magic that will stay with the reader throughout his life.

The Jungle Books are commonly considered Rudyard Kipling's finest work, but he wrote much else that is equally famous, the best of it based on his experience of life in India. He was born there in 1865, the son of J. Lockwood Kipling, an artist of note, and he learned Hindustani from the native nurses who took care of him. He was, of course, sent to England to school; but he returned to become a newspaperman and, with *Plain Tales from the Hills*, to start laying down the foundation of his reputation as a writer. By the time he returned to England to live, in 1889, his name was already widely known. Three years later came a collection of poems, *Barrack Room Ballads*, containing the familiar "If" and "Mandalay," and then *The Jungle Books*, which Kipling wrote during a sojourn in Vermont. They were followed by *Captains Courageous, Kim,* and *Just So Stories*. In 1907 recognition of his now worldwide reputation was signaled by the award of the Nobel Prize for literature—the first such award to an Englishman.

Kipling grew up imbued with an intense, romantic conviction of "the white man's burden"—a phrase, in fact, which he coined—and of the civilizing mission of the British Empire. These themes permeate much of his writing, and time has passed them by. But his vigorous, rhythmic verse is memorable, and certainly any reader of *The Jungle Books* will understand why he is regarded as a master of the short story.

Contents

T WAS SEVEN O'CLOCK of a very warm evening in the Seeonee hills when Father Wolf woke up from his day's rest, scratched himself, yawned, and spread out his paws one after the other to get rid of the sleepy feeling in their tips. Mother Wolf lay with her big gray nose dropped across her four tumbling, squealing cubs, and the moon shone into the mouth of the cave where they all lived. "Augrh!" said Father Wolf, "it is time to hunt again"; and he was going to spring downhill when a little shadow with a bushy tail crossed the threshold and whined: "Good luck go with you, O Chief of the Wolves; and good luck and strong white teeth go with the noble children, that they may never forget the hungry in this world."

It was the jackal—Tabaqui, the Dish-licker—and the wolves of India despise Tabaqui because he runs about making mischief, and telling tales, and eating rags from the village rubbish heaps. But they are afraid of him too, because Tabaqui is apt to go mad, and then he runs through the forest biting everything in his way. Even the tiger runs and hides when little Tabaqui goes mad, for madness—we call it hydrophobia—is the most disgraceful thing that can overtake a wild creature.

"Enter, then, and look," said Father Wolf stiffly; "but there is no food here."

"For a wolf, no," said Tabaqui; "but for so mean a person as myself a dry bone is a good feast. Who are we, the Jackal People, to pick and choose?" He scuttled to the back of the cave, where he found the bone of a buck with some meat on it, and sat cracking the end merrily. "All thanks for this good meal," he said, licking his lips. "How beautiful are the noble children! And so young too! Indeed, the children of kings are men from the beginning."

Now, Tabaqui knew as well as anyone else that there is nothing so unlucky as to compliment children to their faces; and it pleased him to see Mother and Father Wolf look uncomfortable.

Tabaqui sat still, rejoicing in the mischief that he had made; then he said spitefully: "Shere Khan, the Big One, has shifted his hunting grounds. He will hunt among these hills for the next moon, so he has told me."

Shere Khan was the tiger who lived near the Waingunga River, twenty miles away.

"He has no right!" Father Wolf began angrily. "By the Law of the Jungle he has no right to change his quarters without due warning. He will frighten every head of game within ten miles, and I—I have to kill for two, these days."

"His mother did not call him Lungri [the Lame One] for nothing," said Mother Wolf quietly. "He has been lame in one foot from his birth. That is why he has only killed cattle. Now the villagers of the Waingunga are angry with him, and he has come here to make *our* villagers angry. They will scour the Jungle for him when he is far away, and we and our children must run when the grass is set alight. Indeed, we are very grateful to Shere Khan!"

"Shall I tell him of your gratitude?" said Tabaqui.

"Out!" snapped Father Wolf. "Out and hunt with thy master. Thou hast done harm enough for one night."

"I go," said Tabaqui quietly. "Ye can hear Shere Khan below in the thickets. I might have saved myself the message."

Father Wolf listened, and below in the valley that ran down to a little river, he heard the dry, angry, snarly, singsong whine of a tiger who has caught nothing and does not care if all the Jungle knows it.

"The fool!" said Father Wolf. "To begin a night's work with that noise! Does he think that our buck are like his fat Waingunga bullocks?"

"H'sh! It is neither bullock nor buck he hunts tonight," said Mother Wolf. "It is Man." The whine had changed to a sort of humming purr that seemed to come from every quarter of the compass. It was the noise that bewilders woodcutters and gypsies sleeping in the open, and makes them run sometimes into the very mouth of the tiger.

"Man!" said Father Wolf, showing all his white teeth. "Faugh! Are there not enough beetles and frogs in the tanks that he must eat Man, and on our ground too?"

The Law of the Jungle, which never orders anything without a reason, forbids every beast to eat Man except when he is killing to show his children how to kill, and then he must hunt outside the hunting grounds of his pack or tribe. The real reason for this is that man-killing means, sooner or later, the arrival of white men on elephants, with guns, and hundreds of brown men with gongs and rockets and torches. Then everybody in the Jungle suffers. The reason the beasts give among themselves is that Man is the weakest and most defenseless of all living things, and it is unsportsmanlike to touch him. They say too that man-eaters become mangy, and lose their teeth.

The purr grew louder, and ended in the full-throated "Aaarh!" of the tiger's charge.

Then there was a howl—an untigerish howl—from Shere Khan. "He has missed," said Mother Wolf. "What is it?"

Father Wolf ran out a few paces and heard Shere Khan muttering and mumbling savagely, as he tumbled about in the scrub.

"The fool has had no more sense than to jump at a woodcutter's campfire, and has burned his feet," said Father Wolf, with a grunt.

"Something is coming uphill," said Mother Wolf, twitching one ear. "Get ready."

The bushes rustled a little in the thicket, and Father Wolf dropped with his haunches under him, ready for his leap. Then, if you had been watching, you would have seen the most wonderful thing in the world—the wolf checked in mid-spring. He made his bound before he saw what it was he was jumping at, and then he tried to stop himself. The result was that he shot up straight into the air for four or five feet, landing almost where he left ground.

"Man!" he snapped. "A man's cub. Look!"

Directly in front of him, holding on by a low branch, stood a naked brown baby who could just walk—as soft and as dimpled a little atom as ever came to a wolf's cave at night. He looked up into Father Wolf's face and laughed.

"Is that a man's cub?" said Mother Wolf. "I have never seen one. Bring it here."

A wolf accustomed to moving his own cubs can, if necessary, mouth an egg without breaking it, and though Father Wolf's jaws closed right on the child's back not a tooth even scratched the skin, as he laid it down among the cubs.

"How little! How naked, and—how bold!" said Mother Wolf softly. The baby was pushing his way between the cubs to get close to the warm hide. "Ahai! He is taking his meal with the others. Now, was there ever a wolf that could boast of a man's cub among her children?"

"I have heard now and again of such a thing," said Father Wolf. "He is altogether without hair, and I could kill him with a touch of my foot. But see, he looks up and is not afraid."

The moonlight was blocked out of the mouth of the cave, for Shere Khan's great square head and shoulders were thrust into the entrance. Tabaqui, behind him, was squeaking: "My lord, my lord, it went in here!"

"Shere Khan does us great honor," said Father Wolf, but his eyes were very angry. "What does Shere Khan need?"

"My quarry. A man's cub went this way," said Shere Khan. "Give it to me."

Shere Khan had jumped at a woodcutter's campfire, as Father Wolf had said, and was furious from the pain of his burned feet. But Father Wolf knew that the mouth of the cave was too narrow for a tiger to come in by.

"The Wolves are a free people," said Father Wolf. "They take orders from the Head of the Pack, and not from any striped cattle-killer. The man's cub is ours—to kill if we choose."

"What talk is this of choosing? By the Bull that I killed, am I to stand nosing into your dog's den for my fair dues? It is I, Shere Khan, who speak!"

The tiger's roar filled the cave with thunder. Mother Wolf shook herself clear of the cubs and sprang forward, her eyes, like two green moons in the darkness, facing the blazing eyes of Shere Khan.

"And it is I, Raksha [The Demon], who answer. The man's cub is mine. He shall not be killed. He shall live to run with the Pack; and in the end, look you, hunter of little naked cubs—he shall hunt *thee!* Now get hence! Go!"

Father Wolf looked on amazed. He had almost forgotten the days when he won Mother Wolf in fair fight from five other wolves, when she ran in the Pack and was not called The Demon for compliment's sake. Shere Khan might have faced Father Wolf, but he could not stand up against Mother Wolf, for he knew that where he was she had all the advantage of the ground, and would fight to the death. So he backed out of the cave-mouth growling, and when he was clear he shouted: "We will see what the Pack will say to this fostering of man-cubs. The cub is mine, and to my teeth he will come in the end, O bush-tailed thieves!"

Mother Wolf threw herself down panting among the cubs, and Father Wolf said to her gravely: "Shere Khan speaks this much truth. The cub must be shown to the Pack. Wilt thou still keep him, Mother?"

"Keep him!" she gasped. "He came naked, by night, alone and very hungry; yet he was not afraid! Look, he has pushed one of my babes to one side already. Assuredly I will keep him. Lie still, Little Frog. O thou Mowgli—for Mowgli, the Frog, I will call thee—the time will come when thou wilt hunt Shere Khan as he has hunted thee."

"But what will our Pack say?" said Father Wolf.

The Law of the Jungle lays down very clearly that any wolf may, when he marries, withdraw from the Pack he belongs to; but as soon as his cubs are old enough to stand on their feet he must bring them to the Pack Council, which is generally held once a month at full moon, in order that the other wolves may identify them. After that inspection the cubs are free to run where they please, and until they have killed their first buck no excuse is accepted if a grown wolf of the Pack kills one of them. The punishment is death where the murderer can be found; and if you think for a minute you will see that this must be so.

5

Father Wolf waited till his cubs could run a little, and then on the night of the Pack Meeting took them and Mowgli and Mother Wolf to the Council Rock—a hilltop covered with stones and boulders where a hundred wolves could hide. Akela, the great gray Lone Wolf, who led all the Pack by strength and cunning, lay out at full length on his rock, and below him sat forty or more wolves of every size and color, from badger-colored veterans who could handle a buck alone, to young black three-year-olds who thought they could. The Lone Wolf had led them for a year now. He had fallen twice into a wolf trap in his youth, and once he had been beaten and left for dead; so he knew the manners and customs of men. There was very little talking at the Rock. The cubs tumbled over each other in the center of the circle where their mothers and fathers sat, and now and again a senior wolf would go quietly up to a cub, look at him carefully, and return to his place on noiseless feet. Sometimes a mother would push her cub far out into the moonlight, to be sure that he had not been overlooked. Akela from his rock would cry: "Ye know the Law. Look well, O Wolves!" and the anxious mothers would take up the call: "Look—look well, O Wolves!"

At last—and Mother Wolf's neck bristles lifted as the time came—Father Wolf pushed Mowgli, the Frog, into the center, where he sat laughing and playing with some pebbles that glistened in the moonlight.

Akela never raised his head from his paws, but went on with the monotonous cry: "Look well!" A muffled roar came up from behind the rocks—the voice of Shere Khan crying: "The cub is mine. What have the Free People to do with a man's cub?" Akela never even twitched his ears; all he said was: "Look well, O Wolves! What have the Free People to do with the orders of any save the Free People? Look well!"

There was a chorus of deep growls, and a young wolf in his fourth year flung back Shere Khan's question to Akela: "What have the Free People to do with a man's cub?"

Now, the Law of the Jungle lays down that if there is any dispute as to the right of a cub to be accepted by the Pack, he must

6

be spoken for by at least two members of the Pack who are not his father and mother.

"Who speaks for this cub?" said Akela. There was no answer, and Mother Wolf got ready for what she knew would be her last fight, if things came to fighting.

Then the only other creature who is allowed at the Pack Council Baloo, the sleepy brown bear who teaches the wolf cubs the Law of the Jungle: old Baloo, who can come and go where he pleases because he eats only nuts and roots and honey—rose up on his hindquarters and grunted.

"The man's cub?" he said. "*I* speak for him. There is no harm in a man's cub. I have no gift of words, but I speak the truth. Let him run with the Pack, and be entered with the others. I myself will teach him."

"We need yet another," said Akela. "Who speaks besides Baloo?"

A black shadow dropped down into the circle. It was Bagheera, the Black Panther, inky black all over, but with the panther markings showing up in certain lights like the pattern of watered silk. Everybody knew Bagheera, and nobody cared to cross his path; for he was as cunning as Tabaqui, as bold as the wild buffalo, and as reckless as the wounded elephant. But he had a voice as soft as

7

wild honey dripping from a tree, and a skin softer than down.

"O Akela, and ye, the Free People," he purred, "I have no right in your assembly; but the Law of the Jungle says that if there is a doubt in regard to a new cub, the life of that cub may be bought at a price. And the Law does not say who may or may not pay that price. Am I right?"

"Good! Good!" said the young wolves, who are always hungry. "The cub can be bought for a price. It is the Law."

"Knowing that I have no right to speak here, I ask your leave."

"Speak then," cried twenty voices.

"To kill a naked cub is shame. Besides, he may make better sport for you when he is grown. Baloo has spoken in his behalf. Now to Baloo's word I will add one bull, and a fat one, newly killed, if ye will accept the man's cub according to the Law. Is it difficult?"

There was a clamor of scores of voices, saying: "What matter? He will die in the winter rains. He will scorch in the sun. What harm can a naked frog do us? Let him run with the Pack. Where is the bull, Bagheera? Let him be accepted."

And then came Akela's deep bay, crying: "Look well—look well, O Wolves!"

Mowgli was still deeply interested in the pebbles, and he did not notice when the wolves came and looked at him one by one. At last they all went down the hill for the dead bull, and only Akela, Bagheera, Baloo, and Mowgli's own wolves were left. Shere Khan roared still in the night, for he was very angry that Mowgli had not been handed over to him.

"Ay, roar well," said Bagheera, under his whiskers; "for the time comes when this naked thing will make thee roar to another tune, or I know nothing of Man."

"It was well done," said Akela. "Men and their cubs are very wise. He may be a help in time."

"Truly, a help in time of need; for none can hope to lead the Pack forever," said Bagheera.

Akela said nothing. He was thinking of the time that comes to every leader of every pack when his strength goes from him and he gets feebler and feebler, till at last he is killed by the wolves and a new leader comes up—to be killed in his turn.

"Take him away," he said to Father Wolf, "and train him as befits one of the Free People."

And that is how Mowgli was entered into the Seeonee Wolf Pack at the price of a bull and on Baloo's good word.

As THE YEARS WENT BY, Mowgli grew up with the cubs, though they, of course, were grown wolves almost before he was a child. Father Wolf taught him the meaning of things in the Jungle, till every rustle in the grass, every note of the owls above his head, and every splash of every little fish jumping in a pool meant as much to him as the work of his office means to a businessman. When he was not learning, he sat out in the sun and slept, and ate, and went to sleep again; when he felt dirty or hot he swam in the forest pools; and when he wanted honey he climbed up for it, and that Bagheera showed him how to do. Bagheera would lie out on a branch and call, "Come along, Little Brother," and at first Mowgli would cling like the sloth, but afterward he would fling himself through the branches as boldly as a gray ape.

He took his place at the Council Rock, too, when the Pack met, and there he discovered that if he stared hard at any wolf, the wolf would be forced to drop his eyes. At other times he would pick the long thorns out of the pads of his friends, for wolves suffer terribly from thorns and burrs in their coats. He would go down the hillside into the cultivated lands by night, and look very curiously at the villagers in their huts, but he had a mistrust of men because Bagheera showed him a square box with a drop-gate so cunningly hidden in the Jungle that he nearly walked into it, and told him that it was a trap. He loved better than anything else to go with Bagheera into the dark warm heart of the forest, to sleep all through the drowsy day, and at night to see how Bagheera did his killing. Bagheera killed right and left as he felt hungry, and so did Mowgli—with one exception. As soon as he was old enough to understand things, Bagheera told him that he must never touch cattle because he had been bought into the Pack at the price of a bull's life. "All the Jungle is thine," said Bagheera, "and thou canst kill everything that thou art strong enough to kill; but for the sake of the bull that bought thee thou must never kill or eat any cattle. That is the Law of the Jungle." Mowgli obeyed faithfully.

Baloo also taught him the Law of the Jungle. The big, serious, old brown bear was delighted to have so quick a pupil, for the young wolves will only learn as much of the Law as applies to their own pack and tribe, and run away as soon as they can repeat the Hunting Verse: "Feet that make no noise, eyes that can see in the dark, ears that can hear the winds in their lairs, and sharp white teeth—all these things are the marks of our brothers except Tabaqui, the Jackal, and the Hyena whom we hate." But Mowgli, as a man-cub, had to learn a great deal more than this. The boy could climb almost as well as he could swim, and swim almost as well as he could run; so Baloo, the Teacher of the Law, taught him the Wood and Water Laws; how to tell a rotten branch from a sound one; how to speak politely to the wild bees when he came upon a hive of them fifty feet above ground; and how to warn the water snakes in the pools before he splashed down among them. None of the Jungle People like being disturbed, and all are very ready to fly at an intruder. Then, too, Mowgli was taught the Strangers' Hunting Call, which must be repeated till it is answered whenever one of the Jungle People hunts outside his own grounds. It means: "Give me leave to hunt here because I am hungry"; and the answer is: "Hunt then for food, but not for pleasure."

All this will show you how much Mowgli had to learn by heart, and he grew very tired of saying the same thing over a hundred times; but, as Baloo said to Bagheera, the Black Panther, one day when Mowgli had been cuffed and run off in a temper: "A Man-cub is a Man-cub, and he must learn *all* the Law of the Jungle."

"But think how small he is," said the Black Panther, who would have spoiled Mowgli if he had had his own way. "How can his little head carry all thy long talk?"

"Is there anything in the Jungle too little to be killed? No. That is why I teach him these things, and that is why I hit him, very softly, when he forgets."

"Softly! What dost thou know of softness, old Iron-feet?" Bagheera grunted. "His face is all bruised today by thy—softness."

"Better he should be bruised from head to foot by me who love him than that he should come to harm through ignorance," Baloo answered very earnestly. "I am now teaching him the Master Words of the Jungle that shall protect him with the Birds and the Snake People, and all that hunt on four feet. He can now claim protection, if he will only remember the words, from all in the Jungle. Is not that worth a little beating?"

"Well, look to it then that thou dost not kill the Man-cub. But what are those Master Words? I am more likely to give help than to ask it"—Bagheera stretched out one paw and admired the steel-blue, ripping-chisel talons at the end of it—"still I should like to know."

"Mowgli shall say them—if he will. Come, Little Brother!"

"My head is ringing like a bee tree," said a sullen little voice over their heads, and Mowgli slid down a tree trunk, very angry and indignant, adding as he reached the ground: "I come for Bagheera and not for *thee*, fat old Baloo!"

"That is all one to me," said Baloo, though he was hurt and grieved. "Tell Bagheera, then, the Master Words of the Jungle that I have taught thee this day."

"Master Words for which people?" said Mowgli, delighted to show off. "The Jungle has many tongues. *I* know them all."

"A little thou knowest, but not much. See, O Bagheera, they never thank their teacher. Say the Word for the Hunting People, then—great scholar."

"We be of one blood, ye and I," said Mowgli, giving the words the Bear accent which all the Hunting People use.

"Good. Now for the Birds."

Mowgli repeated, with the Kite's whistle at the end of the sentence.

"Now for the Snake People," said Bagheera.

The answer was a perfectly indescribable hiss, and Mowgli kicked up his feet behind, clapped his hands together to applaud himself, and jumped on to Bagheera's back, where he sat sideways, drumming with his heels on the glossy skin and making the worst faces he could think of at Baloo.

"There—there! That was worth a little bruise," said the brown bear tenderly. "Some day thou wilt remember me." Then he turned aside to tell Bagheera how he had begged the Master Words from Hathi, the Wild Elephant, and how Hathi had taken Mowgli down to a pool to get the Snake Word from a water snake, because Baloo could not pronounce it, and how Mowgli was now reasonably safe against all accidents in the Jungle, because neither snake, bird, nor beast would hurt him.

"No one, then, is to be feared," Baloo wound up, patting his big furry stomach with pride.

"Except his own tribe," said Bagheera, under his breath; and then aloud to Mowgli: "Have a care for my ribs, Little Brother! What is all this dancing up and down?"

Mowgli had been trying to make himself heard by pulling at Bagheera's shoulder fur and kicking hard. When the two listened to him he was shouting at the top of his voice: "And so I shall have a tribe of my own, and lead them through the branches all day long."

"What is this new folly, little dreamer of dreams?" said Bagheera.

"Yes, and throw branches and dirt at old Baloo," Mowgli went on. "They have promised me this. Ah!"

"Whoof!" Baloo's big paw scooped Mowgli off Bagheera's back, and as the boy lay looking up from between the big forepaws he could see the Bear was angry.

"Mowgli," said Baloo, "thou hast been talking with the Bandar-log—the Monkey People."

Mowgli looked at Bagheera to see if the Panther was angry too, and Bagheera's eyes were as hard as jadestones.

"Thou hast been with the Monkey People—the people without a Law—the eaters of everything. That is great shame."

"When Baloo hurt my head," said Mowgli, "I went away, and the gray apes came down from the trees and had pity on me. No one else cared." He snuffled a little. "And then, they gave me nuts to eat, and they—they carried me in their arms up to the top of the trees and said I was their blood-brother and should be their leader some day."

"They have *no* leader," said Bagheera. "They lie. They have always lied."

"They were very kind and bade me come again. Why have I never been taken among the Monkey People? They stand on their feet as I do. They do not hit me with hard paws. They play all day. Bad Baloo, let me up! I will play with them again."

"Listen, Man-cub," said the Bear, and his voice rumbled like thunder on a hot night. "I have taught thee all the Law of the Jungle for all the peoples of the Jungle—except the Monkey Folk who live in the trees. They are outcasts. They have no speech of their own, but use the stolen words which they overhear when they listen, and peep, and wait up above in the branches. They are without leaders. They boast that they are a great people about to do great affairs in the Jungle, but the falling of a nut turns their minds to laughter and all is forgotten. We of the Jungle have no dealings with them. Hast thou ever heard me speak of the Bandar-log till today?"

"No," said Mowgli in a whisper, for the forest was very still now that Baloo had finished.

"The Jungle People put them out of their mouths and out of their minds. We do not notice them even when they throw nuts and filth on our heads."

He had hardly spoken when a shower of nuts and twigs spattered down through the branches; and they could hear coughings and howlings and angry jumpings among the thin branches.

The two trotted away, taking Mowgli with them. What Baloo had said about the monkeys was perfectly true. They belonged to the treetops, and as beasts very seldom look up, there was no occasion for the monkeys and the Jungle People to cross each other's path. But whenever they found a sick wolf, or a wounded tiger or bear, the monkeys would torment him. They would howl and shriek senseless songs, and invite the Jungle People to climb up their trees and fight them. None of the beasts could reach them, but on the other hand none of the beasts would notice them, and that was why they were so pleased when Mowgli came to play with them, and when they heard how angry Baloo was.

They never meant to do any more—the Bandar-log never mean anything at all; but one of them invented what seemed to him a brilliant idea, and he told all the others that Mowgli would be a useful person to keep in the tribe, because he could weave sticks together for protection from the wind; so, if they caught him, they could make him teach them. Of course Mowgli, as a woodcutter's child, inherited all sorts of instincts, and used to make little huts of fallen branches without thinking how he came to do it, and the Monkey People, watching in the trees, considered his play most wonderful. This time, they said, they were really going to have a leader and become the wisest people in the Jungle—so wise that everyone else would notice and envy them. Therefore they followed Baloo and Bagheera and Mowgli through the Jungle very quietly till it was time for the midday nap, and Mowgli, who was very much ashamed of himself, slept between the Panther and the Bear, resolving to have no more to do with the Monkey People.

The next thing he remembered was feeling hands on his legs and arms—hard, strong, little hands—and then a swash of branches in his face, and then he was staring down through the swaying boughs as Baloo woke the Jungle with his deep cries and Bagheera bounded up the trunk with every tooth bared. The Bandar-log howled with triumph and scuffled away to the upper branches where Bagheera dared not follow, shouting: "He has noticed us! Bagheera has noticed us! All the Jungle People admire us for our skill and our cunning." Then they began their flight; and the flight of the Monkey People through treeland is one of the things nobody can describe. They have their regular roads and crossroads, up hills and down hills, all laid out from fifty to a hundred feet above ground, and by these they can travel even at night if necessary.

Two of the strongest monkeys caught Mowgli under the arms and swung off with him through the treetops, twenty feet at a bound. Sick and giddy as Mowgli was he could not help enjoying the wild rush, though the glimpses of earth far down below frightened him, and the terrible check and jerk at the end of the swing over nothing but empty air brought his heart between his teeth. His escort would rush him up a tree till he felt the thinnest topmost branches crackle and bend under them, and then with a cough and a whoop would fling themselves into the air outward and downward, and bring up hanging by their hands or their feet to the lower limbs of the next tree. Sometimes he could see for miles and miles across the still green Jungle, as a man on the top of a mast can see for miles across the sea, and then the branches and leaves would lash him across the face, and he and his two guards would be almost down to earth again. So, bounding and crashing and whooping and yelling, the whole tribe of Bandar-log swept along the tree roads with Mowgli their prisoner.

For a time he was afraid of being dropped; then he grew angry but knew better than to struggle; and then he began to think. The first thing was to send back word to Baloo and Bagheera, for, at the pace the monkeys were going, he knew his friends would be left far behind. It was useless to look down, for he could only see the top sides of the branches, so he stared upward and saw, far away in the blue, Chil, the Kite, balancing and wheeling as he kept watch over the Jungle waiting for things to die. Chil saw that the monkeys were carrying something, and dropped a few hundred yards to find out whether their load was good to eat. He whistled with surprise when he saw Mowgli being dragged up to a treetop, and heard him give the Kite call for "We be of one blood, thou and I." The waves of the branches closed over the boy, but Chil balanced away to the next tree in time to see the little brown face come up again. "Mark my trail," Mowgli shouted. "Tell Baloo of the Seeonee Pack and Bagheera of the Council Rock."

"In whose name, Brother?" Chil had never seen Mowgli before, though of course he had heard of him.

"Mowgli, the Frog. Man-cub they call me! Mark my tra—il!"

The last words were shrieked as he was being swung through the air, but Chil nodded and rose up till he looked no bigger than a speck of dust, and there he hung, watching the swaying of the treetops as Mowgli's escort whirled along.

Meantime, Baloo and Bagheera were furious with rage and grief. Bagheera climbed as he had never climbed before, but the thin branches broke beneath his weight, and he slipped down, his claws full of bark.

"Why didst thou not warn the Man-cub?" he roared to poor Baloo, who had set off at a clumsy trot in the hope of overtaking the monkeys. "What was the use of half slaying him with blows if thou didst not warn him?"

"Haste! Oh, haste! We—we may catch them yet!" Baloo panted.

"At this speed! It would not tire a wounded cow. Teacher of the Law—cub beater—a mile of that rolling to and fro would burst thee open. Sit still and make a plan. This is no time for chasing. They may drop him if we follow too close."

"*Whoo!* They may have dropped him already, being tired of carrying him. Who can trust the Bandar-log? Roll me into the hives of the wild bees that I may be stung to death, for I am the most miserable of bears! *Wahooa!* Oh, Mowgli, Mowgli! Why did I not warn thee against the Monkey Folk instead of breaking thy head? Now perhaps I may have knocked the day's lesson out of his mind, and he will be alone in the Jungle without the Master Words."

Baloo clasped his paws over his ears and rolled to and fro, moaning.

"At least he gave me all the Words correctly a little time ago," said Bagheera impatiently. "Baloo, thou hast neither memory nor respect. What would the Jungle think if I, the Black Panther, curled myself up like Ikki, the Porcupine, and howled?"

"What do I care what the Jungle thinks? He may be dead by now."

"Unless they drop him from the branches in sport, or kill him out of idleness, I have no fear for the Man-cub. He is wise and well taught, and above all he has the eyes that make the Jungle

People afraid. But (and it is a great evil) he is in the power of the Bandar-log, and they, because they live in trees, have no fear of any of our people." Bagheera licked one forepaw thoughtfully.

"Fool that I am! Oh, fat, brown, root-digging fool that I am!" said Baloo, uncurling himself with a jerk. "It is true what Hathi, the Wild Elephant, says: 'To each his own fear'; and the Bandar-log fear Kaa, the Rock Snake. The whisper of his name makes their wicked tails cold. Let us go to Kaa."

"What will he do for us? He is not of our tribe, being footless—and with most evil eyes," said Bagheera.

"He is very old and very cunning. Above all, he is always hungry," said Baloo hopefully. "Promise him many goats."

"He sleeps for a full month after he has once eaten. He may be asleep now, and even were he awake, what if he would rather kill his own goats?" Bagheera, who did not know much about Kaa, was naturally suspicious.

"Then in that case, thou and I together, old hunter, might make him see reason." Here Baloo rubbed his faded brown shoulder against the Panther, and they went off to look for Kaa, the Rock Python.

They found him stretched out on a warm ledge in the afternoon sun, admiring his beautiful new coat, for he had been in retirement for the last ten days changing his skin, and now he was very splendid—darting his big blunt-nosed head along the ground, and twisting the thirty feet of his body into fantastic knots and curves, and licking his lips as he thought of his dinner to come.

"He has not eaten," said Baloo, with a grunt of relief, as soon as he saw the beautifully mottled brown and yellow jacket. "Be careful, Bagheera! He is always a little blind after he has changed his skin, and very quick to strike."

Kaa was not a poison snake, but his strength lay in his hug, and when he had once lapped his huge coils round anybody there was no more to be said. "Good hunting!" cried Baloo, sitting up on his haunches. Like all snakes of his breed Kaa was rather deaf, and did not hear the call at first. Then he curled up ready for any accident, his head lowered.

"Good hunting for us all!" he answered. "Oho, Baloo, what dost thou do here? Good hunting, Bagheera! One of us at least needs food. Is there any news of game afoot? I am as empty as a dried well."

"We are hunting," said Baloo carelessly. He knew that you must not hurry Kaa. He is too big.

"Give me permission to come with you," said Kaa. "A blow more or less is nothing to thee, Bagheera or Baloo, but I—I have to wait and wait for days in a wood path and climb half a night on the mere chance of a young ape. Pss-haw! The branches are not what they were when I was young. Rotten twigs and dry boughs are they all."

"Maybe thy great weight has something to do with the matter," said Baloo.

"I am a fair length—a fair length," said Kaa, with a little pride. "I came very near to falling on my last hunt, and the noise of my slipping, for my tail was not tightly wrapped round the tree, waked the Bandar-log, and they called me most evil names."

"Footless, yellow earthworm," said Bagheera under his whiskers, as though he were trying to remember something.

"Sssss! Have they ever called me *that?*" said Kaa.

"Something of that kind it was that they shouted to us last moon, but we never noticed them. They will say anything—even that thou hast lost all thy teeth, and wilt not face anything bigger than a kid, because (they are indeed shameless, these Bandar-log)—because thou art afraid of the he-goat's horns," Bagheera went on sweetly.

Now a snake very seldom shows that he is angry, but Baloo and Bagheera could see the big swallowing muscles on either side of Kaa's throat ripple and bulge. "The Bandar-log have shifted their grounds," he said quietly. "When I came up into the sun today I heard them whooping among the treetops."

"It—it is the Bandar-log that we follow now," said Baloo; but the words stuck in his throat, for that was the first time in his memory that one of the Jungle People had owned to being interested in the doings of the monkeys.

"Beyond doubt, then, it is no small thing that takes two such hunters on the trail of the Bandar-log," Kaa replied courteously, as he swelled with curiosity.

"Indeed," Baloo began, "I am no more than the old and sometimes very foolish Teacher of the Law to the Seeonee wolf cubs, and Bagheera here—"

"Is Bagheera," said the Black Panther, and his jaws shut with a snap, for he did not believe in being humble. "The trouble is this, Kaa. Those nut stealers and pickers of palm leaves have stolen away our Man-cub, of whom thou hast perhaps heard."

"I heard some news from Ikki of a man-thing that was entered into a wolf pack, but I did not believe!"

"But it is true. He is such a Man-cub as never was," said Baloo. "The best and wisest and boldest of Man-cubs—my own pupil, who shall make the name of Baloo famous through all the jungles; and besides, I—we—love him, Kaa."

"Tss! Tss!" said Kaa, shaking his head to and fro. "I also have known what love is. There are tales I could tell that—"

"That need a clear night when we are all well fed to praise properly," said Bagheera quickly. "Our Man-cub is in the hands of the Bandar-log now, and we know that of all the Jungle People they fear Kaa alone."

"They have good reason," said Kaa. "Vain, foolish, and chattering are the monkeys. But a man-thing in their hands is in no good luck. They grow tired of the nuts they pick, and throw them down. That man-thing is not to be envied. They called me also— 'yellow fish,' was it not?"

"Worm—worm—earthworm," said Bagheera, "as well as other things which I cannot now say for shame."

"We must remind them to speak well of their master. Now, whither went they with the cub?"

"The Jungle alone knows. Toward the sunset, I believe," said Baloo. "We had thought that thou wouldst know, Kaa."

"I? How? I take them when they come in my way, but I do not hunt the Bandar-log—or green scum on a water hole, or frogs, for that matter."

"Up, Up! Up, Up! Hillo! Illo! Look up, Baloo of the Seeonee Wolf Pack!"

Baloo looked up to see where the voice came from, and there was Chil, the Kite, sweeping down with the sun shining on the upturned flanges of his wings. He had ranged all over the Jungle looking for the Bear and had missed him in the thick foliage.

"What is it?" said Baloo.

"I have seen Mowgli among the Bandar-log. He bade me tell you. The Bandar-log have taken him beyond the river to the Cold Lairs. They may stay there for a night, or ten nights, or an hour. I have told the bats to watch through the dark time. That is my message. Good hunting, all you below!"

"Full gorge and a deep sleep to you, Chil," cried Bagheera. "I will remember thee in my next kill, and put aside the head for thee alone, O best of kites!"

"It is nothing. The boy held the Master Word. I could have done no less," and Chil circled up again to his roost.

"He has not forgotten to use his tongue," said Baloo, with a chuckle of pride. "To think of one so young remembering the Master Word for the Birds too while he was being pulled across trees!"

"It was most firmly driven into him," said Bagheera. "But I am proud of him, and now we must go to the Cold Lairs."

They all knew where that place was, but few of the Jungle People ever went there, because it was an old deserted city, lost and buried in the Jungle, and beasts seldom use a place that men have once used. Besides, the monkeys lived there as much as they could be said to live anywhere, and no self-respecting animal would come within eyeshot of it except in times of drought, when the half-ruined tanks and reservoirs held a little water.

"It is half a night's journey—at full speed," said Bagheera, and Baloo looked very serious. "I will go as fast as I can," he said anxiously.

"We dare not wait for thee. Follow, Baloo. We must go on the quick-foot—Kaa and I."

"Feet or no feet, I can keep abreast of all thy four," said Kaa shortly. Baloo made one effort to hurry, but had to sit down panting, and so they left him to come on later, while Bagheera hurried forward, at the quick panther canter. Kaa said nothing, but, strive as Bagheera might, the huge Rock Python held level with him. When they came to a hill stream, Bagheera gained, because he bounded across while Kaa swam, his head and two feet of his neck clearing the water; but on level ground Kaa made up the distance.

In the Cold Lairs the Monkey People were not thinking of Mowgli's friends at all. They had brought the boy to the Lost City, and were very pleased with themselves for the time. Mowgli had never seen an Indian city before, and though this was almost a heap of ruins it seemed very wonderful and splendid. Some king had built it long ago on a little hill. You could still trace the stone causeways that led up to the ruined gates where the last splinters of wood hung to the worn, rusted hinges. Trees had grown into and out of the walls; the battlements were tumbled down and decayed, and wild creepers hung out of the windows of the towers on the walls in bushy hanging clumps.

A great roofless palace crowned the hill, and the marble of the courtyards and the fountains was split apart by grasses and young trees, and stained with red and green. From the palace you could see the rows and rows of roofless houses that made up the city, looking like empty honeycombs filled with blackness. The monkeys called the place their city, and pretended to despise the Jungle People because they lived in the forest. And yet they never knew what the buildings were made for nor how to use them. They would sit in circles on the hall of the king's council chamber and scratch for fleas and pretend to be men; or they would run in and out of the roofless houses and collect pieces of plaster and old bricks in a corner, and then break off to play up and down the terraces of the king's garden, where they would shake the rose trees and the oranges in sport to see the fruit and flowers fall. They drank at the tanks and made the water all muddy, and then they fought over it, and then they would all rush together in mobs and shout: "There is no one in the Jungle so wise and good and clever and strong and gentle as the Bandar-log." Then all would begin again till they grew tired of the city and went back to the treetops, hoping the Jungle People would notice them.

Mowgli did not like or understand this kind of life. The monkeys dragged him into the Cold Lairs late in the afternoon, and instead of going to sleep, as Mowgli would have done after a long journey, they joined hands and danced about and sang their foolish songs. One of the monkeys made a speech and told his companions that Mowgli's capture marked a new thing in the history of the Bandar-log, for Mowgli was going to show them how to weave sticks and canes together as a protection against rain and cold. Mowgli picked up some creepers and began to work them in and out, and the monkeys tried to imitate; but in a very few minutes they lost interest.

"I wish to eat," said Mowgli. "Bring me food, or give me leave to hunt here."

Twenty or thirty monkeys bounded away to bring him nuts and wild pawpaws; but they fell to fighting on the road, and it was too much trouble to go back with what was left of the fruit. Mowgli was sore and angry as well as hungry, and he roamed through the empty city giving the Strangers' Hunting Call from time to time, but no one answered him. "All that Baloo has said about the Bandar-log is true," he thought to himself. "They have no Law and no leaders—nothing but foolish words and little picking, thievish hands. So if I am starved or killed here, it will be all my own fault. But I must try to return to my own Jungle. Baloo will surely beat me, but that is better than chasing silly rose leaves with the Bandar-log."

No sooner had he walked to the city wall than the monkeys pulled him back, telling him that he did not know how happy he was, and pinching him to make him grateful. He set his teeth and said nothing, but went with the shouting monkeys to a terrace above the red sandstone reservoirs that were half full of rainwater. There was a ruined summerhouse of white marble in the center of the terrace, built for queens dead a hundred years ago. The domed roof had half fallen in and blocked up the underground passage from the palace by which the queens used to enter; but the walls were made of screens of marble tracery—beautiful milk-white fretwork set with agates and carnelians and jasper and lapis lazuli, and as the moon came up behind the hill it shone through the open-work, casting shadows on the ground like black velvet embroidery.

Sore, sleepy, and hungry as he was, Mowgli could not help laughing when the Bandar-log began, twenty at a time, to tell him how great and wise and strong and gentle they were, and how foolish he was to wish to leave them. "We are great. We are free. We are wonderful!" they shouted. "Now, as you are a new listener and can carry our words back to the Jungle People, we will tell you all about our most excellent selves." The monkeys gathered by hundreds and hundreds on the terrace to listen to their own speakers singing the praises of the Bandar-log. Mowgli nodded and blinked, and said "Yes" when they asked him a question, and his head spun with the noise. "Tabaqui, the Jackal, must have bitten all these people," he said to himself, "and now they have the madness. Do they never go to sleep? Now there is a cloud coming to cover the moon. If it were only a big enough cloud I might try to run away in the darkness. But I am tired."

That same cloud was being watched by two good friends in the ruined ditch below the city wall, for Bagheera and Kaa, knowing well how dangerous the Monkey People were in large numbers, did not wish to run any risks. The monkeys never fight unless they are a hundred to one, and few in the Jungle care for those odds.

"I will go to the west wall," Kaa whispered, "and come down swiftly with the slope of the ground in my favor. They will not throw themselves upon *my* back in their hundreds, but—"

"I know it," said Bagheera. "Would that Baloo were here; but we must do what we can. When that cloud covers the moon I shall go to the terrace. They hold some sort of council there over the boy."

"Good hunting!" said Kaa grimly, and glided away to the west wall. That happened to be the least ruined of any, and the big snake was delayed a while before he could find a way up the stones.

The cloud hid the moon, and as Mowgli wondered what would come next he heard Bagheera's light feet on the terrace. The Black Panther had raced up the slope almost without a sound and was striking right and left among the monkeys, who were seated round Mowgli in circles fifty and sixty deep. There was a howl of fright and rage, and then as Bagheera tripped on the rolling, kicking bodies beneath him, a monkey shouted: "There is only one here! Kill him! Kill!" A scuffling mass of monkeys, biting, scratching, tearing and pulling, closed over Bagheera, while five or six laid hold of Mowgli, dragged him up the wall of the summerhouse and pushed him through the hole of the broken dome. A man-trained boy would have been badly bruised, for the fall was a good fifteen feet, but Mowgli fell as Baloo had taught him to fall, and landed on his feet.

"Stay there," shouted the monkeys, "till we have killed thy friend, and later we will play with thee—if the Poison People leave thee alive."

"We be of one blood, ye and I," said Mowgli, quickly giving the Snake's Call. He could hear rustling and hissing in the rubbish all round him, and gave the Call a second time to make sure.

"Even ssso! Down hoods all!" said half a dozen low voices. (Every ruin in India becomes sooner or later a dwelling place of snakes, and the old summerhouse was alive with cobras.) "Stand still, Little Brother, for thy feet may do us harm."

Mowgli stood as quietly as he could, peering through the open-work and listening to the furious din of the fight round the Black Panther—the yells and chatterings and scufflings, and Bagheera's deep, hoarse cough as he backed and bucked and twisted and plunged under the heaps of his enemies. For the first time since he was born, Bagheera was fighting for his life.

"Baloo must be at hand; Bagheera would not have come alone," Mowgli thought; and then he called aloud: "To the tank, Bagheera! Roll and plunge! Get to the water!"

Bagheera heard, and the cry that told him Mowgli was safe gave him new courage. He worked his way desperately, inch by inch, straight for the reservoirs. Then from the ruined wall nearest the Jungle rose up the rumbling war shout of Baloo. "Bagheera," he shouted, "I am here. I climb! I haste! Wait my coming, O most infamous Bandar-log!" He panted up the terrace only to disappear to the head in a wave of monkeys, but he threw himself squarely on his haunches, and spreading out his forepaws, hugged as many as he could hold, and then began to hit with a regular *bat-bat-bat*, like the flipping strokes of a paddle wheel.

A crash and a splash told Mowgli that Bagheera had fought his way to the tank, where the monkeys could not follow. The Panther lay gasping for breath, his head just out of water, while the monkeys stood three-deep on the red steps, dancing up and down with rage, ready to spring upon him from all sides if he came out to help Baloo. It was then that Bagheera lifted up his dripping chin, and in despair gave the Snake's Call for protection— "We be of one blood, ye and I"—for he believed that Kaa had turned tail at the last minute. Even Baloo, half smothered under the monkeys on the edge of the terrace, could not help chuckling as he heard the Black Panther asking for help.

Kaa had only just worked his way over the west wall, landing with a wrench that dislodged a coping stone into the ditch. He had no intention of losing any advantage of the ground, and coiled and uncoiled himself once or twice, to be sure that every foot of his long body was in working order. All that while the fight with Baloo went on, and the monkeys yelled in the tank around Bagheera, and Mang, the Bat, flying to and fro, carried the news of the great battle over the Jungle, till even Hathi, the Wild Elephant, trumpeted, and, far away, scattered bands of the Monkey Folk woke and came leaping along the tree roads to help their comrades in the Cold Lairs.

Then Kaa came straight, quickly, and anxious to kill. The fighting strength of a python is in the driving blow of his head, backed by all the strength and weight of his body. If you can imagine a battering ram, or a hammer weighing nearly half a ton driven by a cool, quiet mind living in the handle of it, you can roughly imagine what Kaa was like when he fought. A python four or five feet long can knock a man down if he hits him fairly in the chest, and Kaa was thirty feet long. His first stroke was delivered into the heart of the crowd round Baloo—was sent home with shut mouth in silence, and there was no need of a second. The monkeys scattered with cries of "Kaa! It is Kaa! Run! Run!"

Generations of monkeys had been scared into good behavior by the stories their elders told them of Kaa, who could slip along the branches as quietly as moss grows, and steal away the strongest monkey that ever lived. Kaa was everything that the monkeys feared in the Jungle, for none of them could look him in the face, and none had ever come alive out of his hug. And so they ran, stammering with terror, to the walls and the roofs of the houses, and Baloo drew a deep breath of relief. His fur was much thicker than Bagheera's, but he had suffered sorely in the fight. Then Kaa opened his mouth for the first time and spoke one long hissing word, and the far-away monkeys, hurrying to the defense of the Cold Lairs, stayed where they were, cowering, till the loaded branches bent and crackled under them. The monkeys on the walls and the empty houses stopped their cries, and in the stillness that fell upon the city Mowgli heard Bagheera shaking his wet sides as he came up from the tank. Then the clamor broke out again. The monkeys leaped higher up the walls; they clung round the necks of the big stone idols and shrieked as they skipped along the battlements, while Mowgli, dancing in the summerhouse, put his eye to the screenwork and hooted owl-fashion between his front teeth, to show his derision and contempt.

"Get the Man-cub out of that trap; I can do no more," Bagheera gasped. "Let us take the Man-cub and go. They may attack again."

"They will not move till I order them. Stay you sssso!" Kaa hissed, and the city was silent once more. "I could not come before, Brother, but I *think* I heard thee call"—this was to Bagheera.

"I—I may have cried out in the battle," Bagheera answered. "Baloo, art thou hurt?"

"I am not sure that they have not pulled me into a hundred little bearlings," said Baloo gravely, shaking one leg after the other. "Wow! I am sore. Kaa, we owe thee, I think, our lives—Bagheera and I."

"No matter. Where is the Manling?"

"Here, in a trap. I cannot climb out," cried Mowgli. The curve of the broken dome was above his head.

"Take him away. He dances like Mao, the Peacock. He will crush our young," said the cobras inside.

"Hah!" said Kaa, with a chuckle, "he has friends everywhere, this Manling. Stand back, Manling; and hide you, O Poison People. I break down the wall."

Kaa looked carefully till he found a discolored crack in the marble tracery showing a weak spot, made two or three light taps with his head to get the distance, and then, lifting up six feet of his body clear of the ground, sent home half a dozen full-power, smashing blows, nose-first. The screenwork broke and fell away in a cloud of dust and rubbish, and Mowgli leaped through the opening and flung himself between Baloo and Bagheera—an arm round each big neck.

"Art thou hurt?" said Baloo, hugging him softly.

"I am sore, hungry, and not a little bruised; but, oh, they have handled ye grievously, my Brothers! Ye bleed."

"Others also," said Bagheera, licking his lips and looking at the monkey-dead on the terrace and round the tank.

"It is nothing, it is nothing if thou art safe, O my pride of all little frogs!" whimpered Baloo.

"Of that we shall judge later," said Bagheera, in a dry voice that Mowgli did not at all like. "But here is Kaa, to whom we owe the battle and thou owest thy life. Thank him according to our customs, Mowgli."

Mowgli turned and saw the great python's head swaying a foot above his own.

"So this is the Manling," said Kaa. "Very soft is his skin, and he is not so unlike the Bandar-log. Have a care, Manling, that I do not mistake thee for a monkey some twilight."

"We be of one blood, thou and I," Mowgli answered. "I take my life from thee, tonight. My kill shall be thy kill if ever thou art hungry, O Kaa."

"All thanks, Little Brother," said Kaa, though his eyes twinkled. "And what may so bold a hunter kill?"

"I kill nothing—I am too little—but I drive goats toward such as can use them. When thou art empty come to me and see if I speak the truth. I have some skill in these"—he held out his hands—"and if ever thou art in a trap, I may pay the debt which I owe to thee, to Bagheera, and to Baloo, here. Good hunting to ye all, my masters."

"Well said," growled Baloo, for Mowgli had returned thanks very prettily. The python dropped his head lightly for a minute on Mowgli's shoulder. "A brave heart and a courteous tongue," said he. "They shall carry thee far through the Jungle, Manling. But now go hence quickly with thy friends. Go and sleep, for the moon sets, and what follows it is not well that thou shouldst see."

Kaa glided out into the center of the terrace and brought his jaws together with a ringing snap that drew all the monkeys' eyes upon him. "The moon sets," he said. "Is there yet light to see?"

From the walls came a moan like the wind in the treetops: "We see, O Kaa."

"Good. Begins now the Dance—the Dance of the Hunger of Kaa. Sit still and watch."

He turned twice or thrice in a big circle, weaving his head from right to left. Then he began making loops and figures of eight with his body, and soft, oozy triangles that melted into squares and five-sided figures, and coiled mounds, never resting, never hurrying, and never stopping his low, humming song. It grew darker and darker, till at last the dragging, shifting coils disappeared, but they could hear the rustle of the scales.

Baloo and Bagheera stood still as stone, growling in their throats, their neck hair bristling, and Mowgli watched and wondered.

"Bandar-log," said the voice of Kaa at last, "can ye stir foot or hand without my order? Speak!"

"Without thy order we cannot stir foot or hand, O Kaa!"

"Good! Come all one pace closer to me."

The lines of the monkeys swayed forward helplessly, and Baloo and Bagheera took one stiff step forward with them.

"Closer!" hissed Kaa, and they all moved again.

Mowgli laid his hands on Baloo and Bagheera to get them away, and the two great beasts started as though they had been waked from a dream.

"Keep thy hand on my shoulder," Bagheera whispered. "Keep it there, or I must go back—must go back to Kaa. *Aah!*"

"It is only old Kaa making circles on the dust," said Mowgli; "let us go"; and the three slipped off through a gap in the walls to the Jungle.

"*Whoof!*" said Baloo, when he stood under the still trees again. "Never more will I make an ally of Kaa," and he shook himself all over.

"He knows more than we," said Bagheera, trembling. "In a little time, had I stayed, I should have walked down his throat."

"Many will walk by that road before the moon rises again," said Baloo.

"But what was the meaning of it all?" said Mowgli, who did not know anything of a python's powers of fascination. "I saw no more than a big snake making foolish circles till the dark came. And his nose was all sore. Ho! Ho!"

"Mowgli," said Bagheera angrily, "his nose was sore on *thy* account; as my ears and sides and paws, and Baloo's neck and shoulders are bitten on *thy* account. Neither Baloo nor Bagheera will be able to hunt with pleasure for many days."

"It is nothing," said Baloo; "we have the Man-cub again."

"True; but he has cost us heavily in time which might have been spent in good hunting, in wounds, in hair—I am half plucked along my back—and, last of all, in honor. For, remember, Mowgli, I, who am the Black Panther, was forced to call upon Kaa for protection, and Baloo and I were both made stupid as little birds by the Hunger Dance. All this, Man-cub, came of thy playing with the Bandar-log."

"True; it is true," said Mowgli sorrowfully. "I am an evil man-cub, and my stomach is sad in me."

"*Mf!* What says the Law of the Jungle, Baloo?"

Baloo did not wish to bring Mowgli into any more trouble, but he could not tamper with the Law, so he mumbled: "Sorrow never stays punishment. But remember, Bagheera, he is very little."

"I will remember; but he has done mischief, and blows must be dealt now. Mowgli, hast thou anything to say?"

"Nothing. I did wrong. Baloo and thou art wounded. It is just."

Bagheera gave him half a dozen love taps; from a panther's point of view they would hardly have waked one of his own cubs, but for a seven-year-old boy they amounted to a severe beating. When it was all over Mowgli sneezed, and picked himself up without a word. "Now," said Bagheera, "jump on my back, Little Brother, and we will go home."

Mowgli laid his head down on Bagheera's back and slept so deeply that he never waked when he was put down by Mother Wolf's side in the home cave.

Mother Wolf had told Mowgli once or twice that Shere Khan was not a creature to be trusted, and that some day he must kill Shere Khan; but though a young wolf would have remembered that advice every hour, Mowgli forgot it because he was only a boy—though he would have called himself a wolf if he had been able to speak in any human tongue.

Shere Khan was always crossing his path in the Jungle, for as Akela grew older and feebler the lame tiger had come to be great friends with the younger wolves of the Pack, who followed him for scraps, a thing that Akela would never have allowed if he had dared to push his authority to the proper bounds. Then Shere Khan would flatter them and wonder that such fine young hunters were content to be led by a dying wolf and a man's cub. "They tell me," Shere Khan would say, "that at Council ye dare not look him between the eyes"; and the young wolves would growl and bristle.

Bagheera, who had eyes and ears everywhere, knew something of this, and once or twice he told Mowgli that Shere Khan would kill him some day; and Mowgli would laugh and answer: "I have the Pack and I have thee; and Baloo, though he is so lazy, might strike a blow or two for my sake. Why should I be afraid?"

It was one very warm day that a new notion came to Bagheera—born of something that he had heard. Perhaps Ikki, the Porcupine, had told him; but he said to Mowgli as the boy lay with his head on Bagheera's beautiful black skin: "Little Brother, how often have I told thee that Shere Khan is thy enemy?"

"As many times as there are nuts on that palm," said Mowgli, who, naturally, could not count. "What of it? I am sleepy, Bagheera, and Shere Khan is all long tail and loud talk."

"But this is no time for sleeping. Baloo knows it; I know it; and the Pack know it. Tabaqui has told thee, too."

"Ho! Ho!" said Mowgli. "Tabaqui came to me not long ago with some rude talk that I was a naked man's cub and not fit to dig pig-nuts; but I caught Tabaqui by the tail and swung him twice against a palm tree to teach him better manners."

"That was foolishness; for though Tabaqui is a mischief-maker, he would have told thee of something that concerned thee closely. Open those eyes, Little Brother. Shere Khan dare not kill thee in the Jungle; but remember, Akela is very old, and soon the day comes when he cannot kill his buck, and then he will be leader no more. Many of the wolves that looked thee over when thou wast brought to the Council feast are old too, and the young wolves believe that a man-cub has no place with the Pack. In a little time thou wilt be a man."

"And what is a man that he should not run with his brothers?" said Mowgli. "I was born in the Jungle. I have obeyed the Law of the Jungle, and there is no wolf of ours from whose paws I have not pulled a thorn. Surely they are my brothers!"

Bagheera stretched himself at full length and half shut his eyes. "Little Brother," said he, "feel under my jaw."

Mowgli put up his strong brown hand, and just under Bagheera's silky chin, where the giant rolling muscles were all hid by the glossy hair, he came upon a little bald spot.

"There is no one in the Jungle that knows that I, Bagheera, carry that mark—the mark of the collar; and yet, Little Brother, I was born among men, and it was among men that my mother died—in the cages of the King's Palace at Oodeypore. It was because of this that I paid the price for thee at the Council when thou wast a little naked cub. Yes, I too was born among men. They fed me behind bars from an iron pan till one night I felt that I was Bagheera, the Panther, and no man's plaything, and I broke the silly lock with one blow of my paw and came away; and because I had learned the ways of men, I became more terrible in the Jungle than Shere Khan. Is it not so?"

"Yes," said Mowgli; "all the Jungle fears Bagheera—all except Mowgli."

"Oh, *thou* art a man's cub," said the Black Panther, very tenderly; "and even as I returned to my Jungle, so thou must go back at last to the men who are thy brothers—if thou art not killed in the Council."

"But why should any wish to kill me?" said Mowgli.

"Look at me," said Bagheera; and Mowgli looked at him steadily between the eyes. The big panther turned his head away in half a minute.

"*That* is why," he said, shifting his paw on the leaves. "Not even I can look thee between the eyes, and I love thee, Little Brother. The others, they hate thee because their eyes cannot meet thine—because thou hast pulled out thorns from their feet—because thou art a man."

"I did not know these things," said Mowgli sullenly; and he frowned under his heavy black eyebrows.

"What is the Law of the Jungle? Strike first and then give tongue. By thy very carelessness they know that thou art a man. But be wise. It is in my heart that when Akela misses his next kill, the Pack will turn against him and against thee. They will hold a Jungle Council at the Rock, and then—and then—I have it!" said Bagheera, leaping up. "Go thou down quickly to the men's huts in the valley, and take some of the Red Flower which they grow there, so that when the time comes thou mayest have even a stronger friend than I or Baloo or those of the Pack that love thee. Get the Red Flower."

By Red Flower Bagheera meant fire. Every beast lives in deadly fear of it, and invents a hundred ways of describing it.

"The Red Flower," said Mowgli, "that grows outside their huts in the twilight. I will get some."

"There speaks the man's cub," said Bagheera proudly. "Remember that it grows in little pots. Get one swiftly, and keep it by thee for time of need."

"Good!" said Mowgli. "I go. But art thou sure, O my Bagheera"—he slipped his arm round the splendid neck, and looked deep into the big eyes—"art thou sure that all this is Shere Khan's doing?"

"By the Broken Lock that freed me, I am sure, Little Brother."

"Then, by the Bull that bought me, I will pay Shere Khan full tale for this, and it may be a little over," said Mowgli; and he bounded away.

"That is all a man," said Bagheera to himself, lying down again. "Oh, Shere Khan, never was a blacker hunting than that frog hunt of thine ten years ago!"

Mowgli ran far and far through the forest, and his heart was hot in him. He came to the cave as the evening mist rose, and drew breath, and looked down the valley. The cubs were out, but Mother Wolf knew by his breathing that something was troubling her frog.

"What is it, Son?" she said.

"Some bat's chatter of Shere Khan," he called back. "I hunt among the plowed fields tonight," and he plunged downward through the bushes, to the stream at the bottom of the valley. There he checked, for he heard the yell of the Pack hunting and the bellow of a hunted sambar. Then there were bitter howls from the young wolves. "Akela! Akela! Let the Lone Wolf show his strength. Room for the leader of the Pack! Spring, Akela!"

The Lone Wolf must have sprung and missed his hold, for Mowgli heard the snap of his teeth and then a yelp as the sambar knocked him over with his forefoot.

He did not wait for anything more, but dashed on; and the yells grew fainter behind him as he ran into the croplands where the villagers lived.

"Bagheera spoke truth," he panted, as he nestled down in some cattle fodder by the window of a hut. "Tomorrow is one day both for Akela and for me."

Then he pressed his face close to the window and watched the fire on the hearth. He saw the husbandman's wife get up and feed it in the night with black lumps; and when the morning came and the mists were all white and cold, he saw the man's child pick up a wicker pot plastered inside with earth, fill it with lumps of red-hot charcoal, put it under his blanket, and go out to tend the cows in the byre.

"Is that all?" said Mowgli. "If a cub can do it there is nothing to fear"; so he strode round the corner and met the boy, took the pot from his hand and disappeared into the mist while the boy howled with fear.

"They are very like me," said Mowgli, blowing into the pot, as he had seen the woman do. "This thing will die if I do not give it things to eat"; and he dropped twigs and dried bark on the red stuff. Halfway up the hill he met Bagheera with the morning dew shining like moonstones on his coat.

"Akela has missed," said the Panther. "They would have killed him last night, but they needed thee also. They were looking for thee on the hill."

"I was among the plowed lands. I am ready. See!" Mowgli held up the firepot.

"Good! Now, I have seen men thrust a dry branch into that stuff, and presently the Red Flower blossomed at the end of it. Art thou not afraid?"

"No. Why should I fear? I remember how, before I was a wolf, I lay beside the Red Flower, and it was warm and pleasant."

All that day Mowgli sat in the cave tending his firepot and dipping dry branches into it to see how they looked. He found a branch that satisfied him, and in the evening when Tabaqui came to the cave and told him rudely enough that he was wanted at the Council Rock, he laughed till Tabaqui ran away. Then Mowgli went to the Council, still laughing.

Akela, the Lone Wolf, lay by the side of his rock as a sign that the leadership of the Pack was open, and Shere Khan with his following of scrap-fed wolves walked to and fro openly. Bagheera lay close to Mowgli, and the firepot was between Mowgli's knees. When they were all gathered together, Shere Khan began to speak—a thing he would never have dared to do when Akela was in his prime.

"He has no right," whispered Bagheera. "Say so. He is a dog's son. He will be frightened."

Mowgli sprang to his feet. "Free People," he cried, "does Shere Khan lead the Pack? What has a tiger to do with our leadership?"

"Seeing that the leadership is yet open, and being asked to speak—" Shere Khan began.

"By whom?" said Mowgli. "Are we *all* jackals, to fawn on this cattle butcher? The leadership of the Pack is with the Pack alone."

There were yells of "Silence, thou man's cub!" "Let him speak. He has kept our Law!" And at last the seniors of the Pack thundered: "Let the Dead Wolf speak." When a leader of the Pack has missed his kill, he is called the Dead Wolf as long as he lives, which is not long, as a rule.

Akela raised his old head wearily: "Free People, and ye too, jackals of Shere Khan, for many seasons I have led ye to and from the kill, and in all my time not one has been trapped or maimed. Now I have missed my kill. Ye know how that plot was made. Ye know how ye brought me up to an untried buck to make my weakness known. It was cleverly done. Your right is to kill me here on the Council Rock now. Therefore I ask, who comes to make an end of the Lone Wolf? For it is my right, by the Law of the Jungle, that ye come one by one."

There was a long hush, for no single wolf cared to fight Akela to the death. Then Shere Khan roared: "Bah! What have we to do with this toothless fool? It is the Man-cub who has lived too long. Free People, he was my meat from the first. Give him to me. He has troubled the Jungle for ten seasons. Give me the Man-cub, or I will hunt here always, and not give you one bone. He is a man's child, and from the marrow of my bones I hate him!"

Then more than half the Pack yelled: "A man! A man! What has a man to do with us? Let him go to his own place."

"And turn all the people of the village against us?" clamored Shere Khan. "No; give him to me. He is a man, and none of us can look him between the eyes."

Akela lifted his head again, and said: "He has eaten our food. He has driven game for us. He has broken no word of the Law of the Jungle."

"Also, I paid for him with a bull when he was accepted. The worth of a bull is little, but Bagheera's honor is something that he will perhaps fight for," said Bagheera in his gentlest voice.

"A bull paid ten years ago!" the Pack snarled. "What do we care for bones ten years old?"

"Or for a pledge?" said Bagheera, his white teeth bared under his lip. "Well are ye called the Free People!"

"No man's cub can run with the people of the Jungle," howled Shere Khan. "Give him to me!"

"He is our brother in all but blood," Akela went on; "and ye would kill him here! In truth, I have lived too long. Some of ye are eaters of cattle, and of others I have heard that, under Shere Khan's teaching, ye go by dark night and snatch children from the villager's doorstep. Therefore I know ye to be cowards, and it is to cowards I speak. It is certain that I must die, and my life is of no worth, or I would offer that in the Man-cub's place. But for the sake of the Honor of the Pack—a little matter that by being without a leader ye have forgotten—I promise that if ye let the Man-cub go to his own place, I will not, when my time comes to die, bare one tooth against ye. I will die without fighting. That will at least save the Pack three lives. More I cannot do; but if ye will, I can save ye the shame that comes of killing a brother against whom there is no fault—a brother spoken for and bought into the Pack according to the Law of the Jungle."

"He is a man—a man—a man!" snarled the Pack; and most of the wolves began to gather round Shere Khan, whose tail was beginning to switch.

"Now the business is in thy hands," said Bagheera to Mowgli. "*We* can do no more except fight."

Mowgli stood upright—the firepot in his hands. Then he

stretched out his arms, and yawned in the face of the Council; but he was furious with rage and sorrow, for, wolflike, the wolves had never told him how they hated him. "Listen, you!" he cried. "There is no need for this dog's jabber. Ye have told me so often tonight that I am a man (and indeed I would have been a wolf with you to my life's end) that I feel your words are true. So I do not call ye my brothers anymore, but dogs, as a man should. What ye will do, and what ye will not do, is not yours to say. That matter is with *me;* and that we may see the matter more plainly, I, the man, have brought here a little of the Red Flower which ye, dogs, fear."

He flung the firepot on the ground, and some of the red coals lit a tuft of dried moss that flared up as all the Council drew back in terror before the leaping flames.

Mowgli thrust his dead branch into the fire till the twigs lit and crackled, and whirled it above his head among the cowering wolves.

"Thou art the master," said Bagheera, in an undertone. "Save Akela from the death. He was ever thy friend."

Akela, the grim old wolf who had never asked for mercy in his life, gave one piteous look at Mowgli as the boy stood all naked, his long black hair tossing over his shoulders in the light of the blazing branch that made the shadows jump and quiver.

"Good!" said Mowgli, staring round slowly. "I see that ye are dogs. I go from you to my own people—if they be my own people. The Jungle is shut to me, and I must forget your talk and companionship; but I will be more merciful than ye are. Because I was all but your brother in blood, I promise that when I am a man among men I will not betray ye to men as ye have betrayed me." He kicked the fire with his foot, and the sparks flew up. "There shall be no war between any of us and the Pack. But here is a debt to pay before I go." He strode forward to where Shere Khan sat blinking stupidly at the flames, and caught him by the tuft on his chin. Bagheera followed, in case of accidents. "Up, dog!" Mowgli cried. "Up, when a man speaks, or I will set that coat ablaze!"

Shere Khan's ears lay flat back on his head, and he shut his eyes, for the blazing branch was very near.

"This cattle-killer said he would kill me in the Council because he had not killed me when I was a cub. Thus and thus, then, do we beat dogs when we are men. Stir a whisker, Lungri, and I ram the Red Flower down thy gullet!" He beat Shere Khan over the head with the branch, and the tiger whined in an agony of fear.

"Pah! Singed jungle cat—go now! But remember, when next I come to the Council Rock, as a man should come, it will be with Shere Khan's hide on my head. For the rest, Akela goes free to live as he pleases, because that is my will. Nor do I think that ye will sit here any longer, lolling out your tongues as though ye were somebodies, instead of dogs whom I drive out—thus! Go!" The fire was burning furiously at the end of the branch, and Mowgli struck right and left round the circle, and the wolves ran howling with the sparks burning their fur. At last there were only Akela, Bagheera, and perhaps ten wolves that had taken Mowgli's part. Then something began to hurt Mowgli inside him, and he caught his breath and sobbed, and the tears ran down his face.

"What is it? What is it?" he said. "I do not wish to leave the Jungle, and I do not know what this is. Am I dying, Bagheera?"

"No, Little Brother. Those are only tears such as men use," said Bagheera. "Now I know thou art a man. The Jungle is shut indeed to thee henceforward. Let them fall, Mowgli. They are only tears." So Mowgli sat and cried as though his heart would break; and he had never cried in all his life before.

"Now," he said, "I will go to men. But first I must say farewell to my mother"; and he went to the cave where she lived with Father Wolf, and he cried on her coat, while the four cubs howled miserably.

"Ye will not forget me?" said Mowgli.

"Never while we can follow a trail," said the cubs. "Come to the foot of the hill when thou art a man, and we will talk to thee; and we will come into the croplands to play with thee by night."

"Come soon!" said Father Wolf. "Oh, wise Little Frog, come again soon; for we be old, thy mother and I."

"Come soon," said Mother Wolf, "little naked son of mine; for, listen, child of man, I loved thee more than ever I loved my cubs."

"I will surely come," said Mowgli; "and when I come it will be to lay out Shere Khan's hide upon the Council Rock. Do not forget me! Tell them in the Jungle never to forget me!"

THE DAWN WAS BEGINNING TO BREAK when Mowgli went down the hillside to meet those mysterious things that are called men. He kept to the rough road that ran down the valley, and followed it for nearly twenty miles, till he came to a country that he did not know. The valley opened out into a great plain dotted over with rocks and cut up by ravines. At one end stood a little village, and at the other the thick Jungle came down to the grazing grounds, and stopped there as though it had been cut off with a hoe. All over the plain, cattle and buffaloes were grazing, and when the little boys in charge of the herds saw Mowgli they shouted and ran away. Mowgli walked on, for he was feeling hungry, and when he came to the village gate he saw the big thornbush that was drawn up before the gate at twilight pushed to one side.

"Umph!" he said, for he had come across more than one such barricade in his night rambles after things to eat. "So men are afraid of the People of the Jungle here also." He sat down by the gate, and when a man came out he stood up and pointed down his mouth to show that he wanted food. The man stared, and ran back up the one street of the village shouting for the priest, who was a big, fat man dressed in white, with a red and yellow mark on his forehead. The priest came to the gate, and with him at least a hundred people who stared and talked and pointed at Mowgli.

"They have no manners, these Men Folk," said Mowgli to himself. "Only the gray ape would behave as they do." So he threw back his long hair and frowned at the crowd.

"What is there to be afraid of?" said the priest. "Look at the marks on his arms and legs. They are the bites of wolves. He is but a wolf-child run away from the Jungle."

Of course, in playing together, the cubs had often nipped Mowgli harder than they intended, and there were white scars all over his arms and legs. But he would have been the last person in the world to call these bites, for he knew what real biting meant.

"*Arré! Arré!*" said two or three women together. "To be bitten by wolves, poor child! He is a handsome boy. By my honor, Messua, he is not unlike thy boy that was taken by the tiger."

"Let me look," said a woman with heavy copper rings on her wrists and ankles, and she peered at Mowgli under the palm of her hand. "Indeed he is not. He is thinner, but he has the very look of my boy."

The priest was a clever man, and Messua was wife to the richest villager in the place. So he looked up at the sky for a minute, and said solemnly: "What the Jungle has taken the Jungle has restored. Take the boy into thy house, my sister, and forget not to honor the priest who sees so far into the lives of men."

"By the Bull that bought me," said Mowgli to himself, "but all this talking is like another Looking-over by the Pack!"

The crowd parted as the woman beckoned Mowgli to her hut, where there was a red-lacquered bedstead, a great earthen grain chest, half a dozen copper cooking pots, and an image of a Hindu god in a little alcove.

She gave him a long drink of milk and some bread, and then she laid her hand on his head and looked into his eyes; for she thought that perhaps he might be her real son come back from the Jungle. So she said: "Nathoo, O Nathoo!" Mowgli did not show that he knew the name. "Dost thou not remember the day when I gave thee thy new shoes?" She touched his foot, and it was almost as hard as horn. "No," she said sorrowfully, "those feet have never worn shoes, but thou art very like my Nathoo, and thou shalt be my son."

"What is the good of a man," Mowgli said to himself, "if he does not understand man's talk? I must learn this talk."

It was not for fun that he had learned in the Jungle to imitate the challenge of bucks and the grunt of the little wild pig. So as soon as Messua pronounced a word Mowgli would imitate it almost perfectly, and before dark he had learned the names of many things in the hut.

There was a difficulty at bedtime, because Mowgli would not sleep under anything that looked so like a panther trap as that hut, and when they shut the door he went through the window. "Give him his will," said Messua's husband. "Remember he can never till now have slept on a bed."

So Mowgli stretched himself in some long, clean grass at the edge of the field, but before he had closed his eyes a soft gray nose poked him under the chin.

"Phew!" said Gray Brother (he was the eldest of Mother Wolf's cubs). "This is a poor reward for following thee twenty miles. Thou smellest altogether like a man already. Wake, Little Brother; I bring news."

"Are all well in the Jungle?" said Mowgli, hugging him.

"All except the wolves that were burned with the Red Flower. Now, listen. Shere Khan has gone away to hunt far off till his coat grows again, for he is badly singed. When he returns he swears that he will lay thy bones in the Waingunga."

"I also have made a little promise. But news is always good. I am tired tonight—very tired with new things, Gray Brother—but bring me the news always."

"Thou wilt not forget that thou art a wolf?" said Gray Brother anxiously.

"Never. I will always remember that I love thee and all in our cave; but also I will always remember that I have been cast out of the Pack."

"And that thou mayest be cast out of another pack. Men are only men, Little Brother, and their talk is like the talk of frogs in a pond. When I come down here again, I will wait for thee in the bamboos at the edge of the grazing ground."

For three months after that night Mowgli hardly ever left the village gate, he was so busy learning the ways of men. First he had to wear a cloth round him, which annoyed him horribly; and then he had to learn about money, which he did not in the least understand, and about plowing, of which he did not see the use. Then the little children in the village made him very angry. When they made fun of him because he would not play games or fly kites, or because he mispronounced some word, only the knowledge that it was unsportsmanlike to kill little naked cubs kept him from picking them up and breaking them in two.

He did not know his own strength in the least. In the Jungle he knew he was weak compared with the beasts, but in the village people said that he was as strong as a bull.

And Mowgli had not the faintest idea of the difference that caste makes between man and man. When the potter's donkey slipped in the clay pit, Mowgli hauled it out by the tail, and helped to stack the pots for their journey to the market at Khanhiwara. That was very shocking, too, for the potter is a low-caste man, and his donkey is worse. When the priest scolded him, Mowgli threatened to put him on the donkey, too, and the priest told Messua's husband that Mowgli had better be set to work as soon as possible; and the village headman told Mowgli that he would have to go out with the buffaloes next day, and herd them while they grazed. No one was more pleased than Mowgli; and that night, because he had been appointed, as it were, a servant of the village, he went off to a circle that met every evening on a masonry platform under a great fig tree. It was the village club, and the headman and the watchman and the barber, and old Buldeo, the village hunter, who owned a Tower musket, met and smoked their big hookahs [water pipes] till far into the night. They told wonderful tales of gods and men and ghosts; and Buldeo told even more wonderful ones of the ways of beasts in the Jungle, till the eyes of the children sitting outside the circle bulged out of their heads.

Mowgli, who naturally knew something about what they were talking of, had to cover his face not to show that he was laughing, while Buldeo, the Tower musket across his knees, climbed on from one wonderful story to another.

Buldeo was explaining how the tiger that had carried away Messua's son was a ghost tiger, and his body was inhabited by the ghost of a wicked old moneylender, who had died some years ago. "And I know that this is true," he said, "because Purun Dass always limped, and the tiger that I speak of, *he* limps, too."

"True, true; that must be the truth," said the graybeards, nodding together.

"Are all these tales such cobwebs and moon talk?" said Mowgli. "That tiger limps because he was born lame, as everyone knows. To talk of the soul of a moneylender in a beast that never had the courage of a jackal is child's talk."

Buldeo was speechless with surprise for a moment, and the headman stared.

"Oho! It is the Jungle brat, is it?" said Buldeo. "If thou art so wise, better bring his hide to Khanhiwara, for the Government has set a hundred rupees on his life. Better still, do not talk when thy elders speak."

Mowgli rose to go. "All the evening I have lain here listening," he called back over his shoulder, "and, except once or twice, Buldeo has not said one word of truth concerning the Jungle, which is at his very doors."

"It is full time that boy went to herding," said the headman, while Buldeo puffed and snorted at Mowgli's impertinence.

The custom of most Indian villages is for a few boys to take the cattle and buffaloes out to graze in the early morning, and bring them back at night; and the very cattle that would trample a white man to death allow themselves to be bullied and shouted at by children that hardly come up to their noses. So long as the boys keep with the herds they are safe, for not even the tiger will charge a mob of cattle. But if they straggle to pick flowers or hunt lizards, they are sometimes carried off. Mowgli went through the village street in the dawn, sitting on the back of Rama, the great herd bull; and the slaty-blue buffaloes, with their long, backward-sweeping horns and savage eyes, rose out of their byres, one by one, and followed him, and Mowgli made it very clear to the children with him that he was the master.

43

An Indian grazing ground is all rocks and scrub and little ravines, among which the herds scatter and disappear. The buffaloes generally keep to the pools and muddy places, where they lie wallowing in the warm mud for hours. Mowgli drove them on to the edge of the plain where the Waingunga River came out of the Jungle; then he dropped from Rama's neck, trotted off to a bamboo clump, and found Gray Brother. "Ah!" said Gray Brother. "I have waited here very many days. What is the meaning of this cattle-herding work?"

"It is an order," said Mowgli. "What news of Shere Khan?"

"He has come back to this country, and has waited here a long time for thee. Now he has gone off again, for the game is scarce. But he means to kill thee."

"Very good," said Mowgli. "So long as he is away do thou or one of the four brothers sit on that rock, so that I can see thee as I come out of the village. When he comes back wait for me in the ravine by the dhak tree in the center of the plain. We need not walk into Shere Khan's mouth."

Then Mowgli picked out a shady place, and lay down and slept while the buffaloes grazed round him. Herding in India is one of the laziest things in the world. The cattle move and crunch, and lie down, and move on again, and they do not even low. They only grunt, and the buffaloes very seldom say anything, but get down into the muddy pools one after another, and work their way into the mud till only their noses and staring china-blue eyes show above the surface, and there they lie like logs. Then the children sleep and wake and sleep again, and weave little baskets of dried grass and put grasshoppers in them; or string a necklace of red and black Jungle nuts; or watch a snake hunting a frog near the wallows. Then they sing long, long songs, and the day seems longer than most people's whole lives. Then evening comes, and the children call, and the buffaloes lumber up out of the sticky mud with noises like gunshots going off one after the other, and they all string across the gray plain back to the twinkling village lights.

Day after day Mowgli would lead the buffaloes out, and day

after day he would see Gray Brother's back a mile and a half away across the plain (so he knew that Shere Khan had not come back). At last a day came when he did not see Gray Brother at the signal place, and he laughed and headed the buffaloes for the ravine by the dhak tree, which was all covered with golden-red flowers. There sat Gray Brother, every bristle on his back lifted.

"He has hidden for a month to throw thee off thy guard. He crossed the ranges last night with Tabaqui, hotfoot on thy trail," said the wolf, panting.

Mowgli frowned. "I am not afraid of Shere Khan, but Tabaqui is very cunning."

"Have no fear," said Gray Brother, licking his lips a little. "I met Tabaqui in the dawn. He told me everything before I broke his back. Shere Khan's plan is to wait for thee at the village gate this evening. He is lying up now in the big dry ravine of the Waingunga."

"Has he eaten today, or does he hunt empty?" said Mowgli, for the answer meant life or death to him.

"He killed at dawn—a pig—and he has drunk too. Remember, Shere Khan could never fast, even for the sake of revenge."

"Oh! Fool, fool! Eaten and drunk too, and he thinks that I shall wait till he has slept! Now, where does he lie up? If there were but ten of us we might pull him down as he lies. These buffaloes will not charge unless they wind him, and I cannot speak their language. Can we get behind his track so that they may smell it?"

"He swam far down the Waingunga to cut that off," said Gray Brother.

"Tabaqui told him that, I know. He would never have thought of it alone." Mowgli stood with his finger in his mouth, thinking. "The big ravine of the Waingunga opens out on the plain not half a mile from here. I can take the herd round through the Jungle to the head of the ravine and then sweep down—but he would slink out at the foot. We must block that end. Gray Brother, canst thou cut the herd in two for me?"

"Not I, perhaps—but I have brought a wise helper." Gray

Brother trotted off and dropped into a hole. Then there lifted up a huge gray head that Mowgli knew well, and the hot air was filled with the most desolate cry of all the Jungle—the hunting howl of a wolf at midday.

"Akela! Akela!" said Mowgli, clapping his hands. "I might have known that thou wouldst not forget me. We have a big work in hand. Cut the herd in two, Akela. Keep the cows and calves together, and the bulls and the plow-buffaloes by themselves."

The two wolves ran in and out of the herd, which snorted and threw up their heads, and separated into two clumps. In one the cow-buffaloes stood, with their calves in the center, and glared and pawed, ready, if a wolf would only stay still, to charge down and trample the life out of him. In the other the bulls snorted and stamped; but, though they looked more imposing, they were much less dangerous, for they had no calves to protect.

"What orders?" panted Akela. "They are trying to join again."

Mowgli slipped on to Rama's back. "Drive the bulls away to the left, Akela. Gray Brother, when we are gone, hold the cows together, and drive them into the foot of the ravine."

"How far?" said Gray Brother, panting and snapping.

"Till the sides are higher than Shere Khan can jump," shouted Mowgli. The bulls swept off as Akela bayed, and Gray Brother stopped in front of the cows. They charged down on him, and he ran just before them to the foot of the ravine.

"Well done! Another charge and they are fairly started. Careful, now—careful, Akela. A snap too much, and the bulls will charge."

"Shall I turn them into the Jungle?" gasped Akela in the dust.

"Ay, turn them! Rama is mad with rage. Oh, if I could only tell him what I need of him today!"

The bulls were turned to the right this time, and crashed into the standing thicket. The other herd children, watching with the cattle half a mile away, hurried to the village as fast as their legs could carry them, crying that the buffaloes had gone mad and run away.

But Mowgli's plan was simple enough. All he wanted to do was to make a big circle uphill and get at the head of the ravine, and then take the bulls down it and catch Shere Khan between the bulls and the cows; for he knew that after a meal and a full drink Shere Khan would not be in any condition to fight or to clamber up the sides of the ravine. He was soothing the buffaloes now by voice, and Akela had dropped far to the rear. It was a long, long circle, for they did not wish to get too near and give Shere Khan warning. At last Mowgli rounded up the bewildered herd at the head of the ravine on a grassy patch that sloped steeply down to the ravine itself. Mowgli looked down at the sides of the ravine, and he saw with a great deal of satisfaction that they ran nearly straight up and down, while the creepers that hung over them would give no foothold to a tiger who wanted to get out.

"Let them breathe, Akela," he said, holding up his hand. "They have not winded him yet. I must tell Shere Khan who comes. We have him in the trap."

He put his hands to his mouth and shouted down the ravine— it was almost like shouting down a tunnel—and the echoes jumped from rock to rock.

After a long time there came back the drawling, sleepy snarl of a full-fed tiger just wakened.

"Who calls?" said Shere Khan, and a splendid peacock fluttered up out of the ravine, screeching.

"I, Mowgli. Cattle thief, it is time to come to the Council Rock! Down—hurry them down, Akela! Down, Rama, down!"

The herd paused for an instant at the edge of the slope, but Akela gave tongue in the full hunting yell, and they pitched over one after the other, the sand and stones spurting up round them. Once started, there was no chance of stopping, and before they were fairly in the bed of the ravine Rama winded Shere Khan and bellowed.

"Ha! Ha!" said Mowgli, on his back. "Now thou knowest!" and the torrent of black horns, foaming muzzles, and staring eyes whirled down the ravine like boulders in floodtime. The buffaloes knew what the business was before them—the terrible charge of the herd, against which no tiger can hope to stand. Shere Khan heard the thunder of their hoofs, picked himself up, and lumbered down the ravine, looking for some way of escape; but the walls of the ravine were straight, and he had to keep on, heavy with his dinner and his drink, willing to do anything rather than fight. The herd splashed through the pool he had just left, bellowing till the narrow cut rang. Mowgli heard an answering bellow from the foot of the ravine, saw Shere Khan turn (the tiger knew it was better to meet the bulls than the cows with their calves), and then Rama tripped, stumbled, and went on again over something soft, and, with the bulls at his heels, crashed full into the other herd, while the weaker buffaloes were lifted clean off their feet by the shock of the meeting. That charge carried both herds out into the plain, goring and stamping and snorting. Mowgli watched his time, and slipped off Rama's neck, laying about him right and left with his stick.

"Quick, Akela! Break them up, or they will be fighting one another. Drive them away, Akela. *Hai! hai! hai!* my children. Softly now, softly! It is all over."

Akela and Gray Brother ran to and fro nipping the buffaloes' legs, and though the herd wheeled once to charge up the ravine again, Mowgli managed to turn Rama, and the others followed him to the wallows.

Shere Khan needed no more trampling. He was dead, and the kites were coming for him already.

"Brothers, that was a dog's death," said Mowgli, feeling for the knife he always carried in a sheath round his neck now that he lived with men. "But he would never have shown fight. His hide will look well on the Council Rock. We must get to work swiftly."

A boy trained among men would never have dreamed of skinning a ten-foot tiger alone, but Mowgli knew better than anyone else how an animal's skin is fitted on. But it was hard work, and Mowgli slashed and tore and grunted for an hour, while the wolves came forward and tugged as he ordered them.

Presently a hand fell on his shoulder, and looking up he saw Buldeo with the Tower musket. The children had told the village about the buffalo stampede, and Buldeo went out angrily, only too anxious to correct Mowgli for not taking better care of the herd.

The wolves dropped out of sight as soon as they saw the man coming.

"What is this folly?" said Buldeo angrily. "To think that thou canst skin a tiger! Where did the buffaloes kill him? It is the Lame Tiger, too, and there is a hundred rupees on his head. Well, well, we will overlook thy letting the herd run off, and perhaps I will give thee one of the rupees of the reward when I have taken the skin to Khanhiwara." He fumbled in his waistcloth for flint and steel, and stooped to singe Shere Khan's whiskers. Most native hunters singe a tiger's whiskers to prevent his ghost haunting them.

"Hum!" said Mowgli, half to himself as he ripped back the skin of a forepaw. "So thou wilt take the hide to Khanhiwara for the reward, and perhaps give me one rupee? Now it is in my mind that I need the skin for my own use. Heh! old man, take away that fire!"

"What talk is this to the chief hunter of the village? Thy luck and the stupidity of thy buffaloes have helped thee to this kill. The tiger has just fed, or he would have gone twenty miles by this time. Thou canst not even skin him properly, little beggar brat. Mowgli, I will not give thee one anna of the reward, but only a very big beating."

"By the Bull that bought me," said Mowgli, who was trying to get at the shoulder, "must I stay babbling to an old ape all noon? Here, Akela, this man plagues me."

Buldeo, who was still stooping over Shere Khan's head, found himself sprawling on the grass, with a gray wolf standing over him, while Mowgli went on skinning as though he were alone in all India.

"Ye—es," he said, between his teeth. "Thou art altogether right, Buldeo. Thou wilt never give me one anna of the reward. There is an old war between this lame tiger and myself—a very old war, and—I have won."

To do Buldeo justice, if he had been ten years younger he would have taken his chance with Akela had he met the wolf in the woods; but a wolf who obeyed the orders of this boy was not a common animal. It was magic of the worst kind, thought Buldeo, and he wondered whether the amulet round his neck would protect him. He lay as still as still, expecting every minute to see Mowgli turn into a tiger, too.

"Maharaj! Great King!" he said at last, in a husky whisper.

"Yes," said Mowgli, without turning his head, chuckling a little.

"I am an old man. I did not know that thou wast anything more than a herdboy. May I rise up and go away, or will thy servant tear me to pieces?"

"Go, and peace go with thee. Only, another time do not meddle with my game. Let him go, Akela."

Buldeo hobbled away to the village as fast as he could. When he got there he told a tale of magic and sorcery that made the priest look very grave.

Mowgli went on with his work, but it was nearly twilight before he and the wolves had drawn the great gay skin clear of the body.

"Now we must hide this and take the buffaloes home! Help me to herd them, Akela."

The herd rounded up in the misty twilight, and when they got near the village Mowgli saw lights, and heard the conches and bells blowing and banging. Half the village seemed to be waiting for him by the gate. "That is because I have killed Shere Khan," he said to himself; but a shower of stones whistled about his ears, and the villagers shouted: "Sorcerer! Wolf's brat! Get hence quickly, or the priest will turn thee into a wolf again. Shoot, Buldeo, shoot!"

The old Tower musket went off with a bang, and a young buffalo bellowed in pain.

"More sorcery!" shouted the villagers. "He can turn bullets. Buldeo, that was *thy* buffalo."

"Now what is this?" said Mowgli, bewildered, as the stones flew thicker.

"They are not unlike the Pack, these brothers of thine," said Akela, sitting down composedly. "It is in my head that they would cast thee out."

"Wolf! Wolf's cub! Go away!" shouted the priest, waving a sprig of the sacred tulsi plant.

"Again? Last time it was because I was a man. This time it is because I am a wolf. Let us go, Akela."

Messua ran across to the herd, and cried: "Oh, my son, my son! They say thou art a sorcerer who can turn himself into a beast at will. I do not believe, but go away or they will kill thee. Buldeo says thou art a wizard, but I know thou hast avenged Nathoo's death."

"Come back, Messua!" shouted the crowd. "Come back, or we will stone thee."

Mowgli laughed a little short ugly laugh, for a stone had hit him in the mouth. "Run back, Messua. This is one of the foolish tales they tell under the big tree at dusk. I have at least paid for thy son's life. Farewell; and run quickly, for I shall send the herd in more swiftly than their brickbats. Farewell!"

"Now, Akela," he cried. "Bring the herd in."

The buffaloes were anxious enough to get to the village. They hardly needed Akela's yell, but charged through the gate like a whirlwind, scattering the crowd right and left.

"Keep count!" shouted Mowgli scornfully. "It may be that I have stolen one of them. Keep count, for I will do your herding no more. Fare you well, children of men, and thank Messua that I do not come in with my wolves and hunt you up and down your streets."

He turned on his heel and walked away with the Lone Wolf; and as he looked up at the stars he felt happy. "No more sleeping in traps for me, Akela. Let us get Shere Khan's skin and go away. No; we will not hurt the village, for Messua was kind to me."

As the moon rose over the plain, the horrified villagers saw Mowgli, with two wolves at his heels and a bundle on his head, trotting across at the steady wolf's trot that eats up the long miles like fire. Then they banged the temple bells and blew the conches louder than ever; and Messua cried, and Buldeo embroidered the story of his adventures in the Jungle.

The moon was just going down when Mowgli and the two wolves came to the hill of the Council Rock, and they stopped at Mother Wolf's cave.

"They have cast me out from the Man Pack, Mother," shouted Mowgli, "but I come with the hide of Shere Khan to keep my word." Mother Wolf walked stiffly from the cave with the cubs behind her, and her eyes glowed as she saw the skin.

"I told him on that day, when he crammed his head and shoulders into this cave, hunting for thy life, Little Frog—I told him that the hunter would be the hunted. It is well done."

"Little Brother, it is well done," said a deep voice in the thicket. "We were lonely in the Jungle without thee," and Bagheera came running to Mowgli's feet. They clambered up the Council Rock together, and Mowgli spread the skin out on the flat stone where Akela used to sit, and pegged it down with four slivers of bamboo, and Akela lay down upon it, and called the old call to the Council, "Look—look well, O Wolves!" exactly as he had called when Mowgli was first brought there.

Ever since Akela had been deposed, the Pack had been without a leader, hunting and fighting at their own pleasure. But they answered the call from habit, and some of them were lame from the traps they had fallen into, and some limped from shot wounds, and many were missing; but they came to the Council Rock, and saw Shere Khan's striped hide on the Rock, and the huge claws dangling at the end of the empty, dangling feet. It was then that Mowgli made up a song, without any rhymes, a song that came up into his throat all by itself, and he shouted it aloud, leaping up and down on the skin, and beating time with his heels till he had no more breath left, while Gray Brother and Akela howled between the verses.

"Look well, O Wolves! Have I kept my word?" said Mowgli when he had finished; and the wolves bayed "Yes," and one tattered wolf howled: "Lead us again, O Akela. Lead us again, O Man-cub, for we be sick of this lawlessness, and we would be the Free People once more."

"Nay," purred Bagheera, "that may not be. When ye are full-fed, the madness may come upon ye again. Not for nothing are ye called the Free People. Ye fought for freedom, and it is yours. Eat it, O Wolves."

"Man Pack and Wolf Pack have cast me out," said Mowgli. "Now I will hunt alone in the Jungle."

"And we will hunt with thee," said the four cubs.

So Mowgli went away and hunted with the four cubs in the Jungle from that day on.

TIME PASSED IN THE JUNGLE. Father and Mother Wolf died, and Mowgli rolled a big boulder against the mouth of their cave, and cried the Death Song over them; Baloo grew very old and stiff, and even Bagheera, whose nerves were steel and whose muscles were iron, was a shade slower on the kill than he had been. Akela turned from gray to milky white with pure age; he walked as though he had been made of wood, and Mowgli killed for him. But the young wolves, the children of the disbanded Seeonee Pack, throve and increased, and when there were about forty of them, Akela told them that they ought to gather themselves together and run under one head, as befitted the Free People.

This was not a question in which Mowgli concerned himself, but when Phao, son of Phaona, fought his way to the leadership of the Pack, according to the Jungle Law, Mowgli came to the Council Rock for memory's sake. When he chose to speak the Pack waited till he had finished, and he sat at Akela's side on the rock above Phao. Those were days of good hunting and good sleeping. The young wolves grew fat and strong, and there were many cubs to bring to the Looking-over. Mowgli always attended a Looking-over, remembering the night when a black panther bought a naked brown baby into the pack, and the long call, "Look—look well, O Wolves," made his heart flutter. Otherwise, he would be far away in the Jungle with his four brothers, tasting, touching, seeing, and feeling new things.

One twilight when he was trotting leisurely across the ranges to give Akela the half of a buck that he had killed, while the Four jogged behind him, tumbling one another over for joy of being alive, he heard a cry that had never been heard since the bad days of Shere Khan. It was what they call in the Jungle the *pheeal*, a hideous kind of shriek that the jackal gives when he is hunting behind a tiger, or when there is a big killing afoot. If you can imagine a mixture of hate, triumph, fear, and despair, with a kind of leer running through it, you will get some notion of the *pheeal*. The Four stopped at once, bristling and growling. Mowgli's hand went to his knife, and his eyebrows knotted.

"There is no Striped One dare kill here," he said.

"That is not the cry of the Forerunner," answered Gray Brother. "It is some great killing. Listen!"

It broke out again, half sobbing and half chuckling, just as though the jackal had soft human lips. Then Mowgli drew a deep breath, and ran to the Council Rock, overtaking on his way hurrying wolves of the Pack. Phao and Akela were on the Rock together, and below them, every nerve strained, sat the others. The mothers and the cubs were cantering off to their lairs; for when the *pheeal* cries it is no time for weak things to be abroad.

They could hear nothing except the Waingunga gurgling in the dark, and the light evening winds among the treetops, till suddenly across the river a wolf called. It was no wolf of the Pack, for they were all at the Rock. The note changed to a long, despairing bay; and "Dhole!" it said. "Dhole! Dhole! Dhole!" They heard tired feet on the rocks, and a gaunt wolf, streaked with red on his flanks, his right forepaw useless and his jaws white with foam, flung himself into the circle and lay gasping at Mowgli's feet.

"Good hunting! Under whose Headship?" said Phao gravely.

"Good hunting! Won-tolla am I," was the answer. He meant that he was a solitary wolf, fending for himself, his mate, and his cubs in some lonely lair, as do many wolves in the south. Won-tolla means an Outlier—one who lies out from any Pack.

"What moves?" said Phao, for that is the question all the Jungle asks after the *pheeal* cries.

"The dhole of the Deccan—Red Dog, the Killer! They came up

from the south saying the Deccan was empty and killing out by the way. When this moon was new there were four to me—my mate and three cubs. At midnight I heard them together, full tongue on the trail. At the dawn wind I found them stiff in the grass—four, Free People, four when this moon was new. Then sought I my Blood Right and found the dhole."

"How many?" said Mowgli quickly; the Pack growled deep in their throats.

"I do not know. Three of them will kill no more, but at the last they drove me like the buck; on my three legs they drove me. Look, Free People!"

He thrust out his mangled forefoot, all dark with dried blood. There were cruel bites low down on his side, and his throat was torn and worried.

"Eat," said Akela, rising up from the meat Mowgli had brought him, and the Outlier flung himself on it.

"This shall be no loss," he said humbly, when he had taken off the first edge of his hunger. "Give me a little strength, Free People, and I also will kill."

Phao heard his teeth crack on a haunch bone and grunted approvingly.

"We shall need those jaws," said he. "Were there cubs with the dhole?"

"Nay, nay. Grown dogs all, heavy and strong for all that they eat lizards in the Deccan."

What Won-tolla had said meant that the red hunting dog of the Deccan was moving to kill, and the Pack knew well that even the tiger will surrender a new kill to the dhole. They drive straight through the Jungle, and what they meet they pull down and tear to pieces. Though they are not as big nor half as cunning as the wolf, they are very strong and very numerous. The dholes, for instance, do not begin to call themselves a pack till they are a hundred strong; whereas forty wolves make a very fair pack indeed. Mowgli's wanderings had taken him to the edge of the high grassy downs of the Deccan, and he had seen the fearless dholes sleeping and playing in the little hollows and tussocks that they use for lairs. He despised them because they did not smell like the Free People, because they did not live in caves, and, above all, because they had hair between their toes while he and his friends were clean-footed. But he knew what a terrible thing a dhole hunting pack was.

Akela knew something of the dholes, too, for he said to Mowgli quietly, "It is better to die in a Full Pack than leaderless and alone. This is good hunting, and—my last. But, as men live, thou hast very many more nights and days, Little Brother. Go north and lie down, and if any live after the dhole has gone by he shall bring thee word of the fight."

"Ah," said Mowgli, quite gravely, "must I go to the marshes and catch little fish and sleep in a tree, or ask help of the Bandar-log and crack nuts, while the Pack fight below?"

"It is to the death," said Akela. "Thou hast never met the Red Killer. Even the Striped One—"

"*Aowa! Aowa!*" said Mowgli pettingly. "I have killed one striped ape, and sure am I in my stomach that Shere Khan would have left his own mate for meat to the dhole if he had winded a pack across three ranges. Listen now: There was a wolf, my father, and there was a wolf, my mother, and there was an old gray wolf (not too wise; he is white now) was my father and my mother. Therefore I—" he raised his voice "—I say that when the dhole come, Mowgli and the Free People are of one skin for that hunting; and I say, by the Bull Bagheera paid for me in the old days which ye of the Pack do not remember, *I* say that this my knife shall be as a tooth to the Pack—and I do not think it is so blunt. This is my Word which has gone from me."

"Thou dost not know the dhole, man with a wolf's tongue," said Won-tolla. "I look only to clear the Blood Debt against them ere they have me in many pieces. But for *ye*, Free People, my word is that ye go north and eat but little for a while till the dhole are gone."

"Hear the Outlier!" said Mowgli with a laugh. "Free People, we must go north and dig lizards and rats from the bank, lest by any chance we meet the dhole. He must kill out our hunting grounds,

Generations of monkeys had been scared into good behavior by the stoires their elders told them of Kaa, who could slip along the branches as quietly as moss grows, and steal away the strongest monkey that ever lived.

Bagheera lay close to Mowgli, and the firepot was between Mowgli's knees.

After a long time there came back the drawling, sleepy snarl of a full-fed tiger just wakened.

Very carefully and gently Mowgli raised Akela to his feet, both arms round him, and the Lone Wolf drew a long breath, and began the Death Song that a leader of the Pack should sing when he dies.

THE WHITE SEAL

RIKKI-TIKKI-TAVI

TOOMAI OF THE ELEPHANTS

THE MIRACLE OF PURUN BHAGAT

while we lie hid till it please him to give us our own again. He is a dog—red, yellow-bellied, lairless, and haired between every toe. Ye know the saying: 'North are the vermin; south are the lice. *We* are the Jungle.' Choose ye, O choose. It is good hunting! For the Pack, for the lair and the litter; for the mate that drives the doe and the little, little cub within the cave; it is met! it is met! it is met!"

The Pack answered with one deep, crashing bark that sounded in the night like a big tree falling. "It is met!" they cried.

"Stay with these," said Mowgli to the Four. "We shall need every tooth. Phao and Akela must make ready the battle. I go to count the dogs. Good hunting all!"

He hurried off into the darkness, wild with excitement, hardly looking where he set foot, and the natural consequence was that he tripped full length over Kaa's great coils where the python lay watching a deer path near the river.

"*Kssha!*" said Kaa angrily. "Is this Jungle work, to stamp and tramp and undo a night's hunting—when the game are moving so well, too?"

"The fault was mine," said Mowgli, picking himself up. "Indeed I was seeking thee, Flathead, but each time we meet thou art longer and broader by the length of my arm. There is none like thee in the Jungle, wise, old, strong, and most beautiful Kaa." And he sat down among the painted coils.

"Now whither does *this* trail lead?" Kaa's voice was gentler. "Not a moon since there was a Manling with a knife threw stones at my head and called me bad little tree-cat names, because I lay asleep in the open."

Kaa made a sort of soft half-hammock of himself under Mowgli's weight. The boy reached out in the darkness, and gathered in the supple cablelike neck till Kaa's head rested on his shoulder, and then he told him all that had happened in the Jungle that night.

"Wise I may be," said Kaa at the end; "but deaf I surely am. Else I should have heard the *pheeal*. How many be the dhole?"

"I have not yet seen. I came hotfoot to thee. But oh, Kaa"—here Mowgli wriggled with sheer joy—"it will be good hunting. Few of us will see another moon."

57

"Dost *thou* strike in this? Remember thou art a Man; and remember what Pack cast thee out. Let the Wolf look to the Dog. *Thou* art a Man."

"Last year's nuts are this year's black earth," said Mowgli. "It is true that I am a Man, but it is in my stomach that this night I have said that I am a Wolf. I am of the Free People, Kaa, till the dhole has gone by."

"Free People," Kaa grunted. "Thou hast tied thyself into the death knot for the sake of the memory of the dead wolves?"

"It is my Word which I have spoken. Till the dhole have gone by my Word comes not back to me."

"*Ngssh!* I had thought to take thee away with me to the northern marshes, but the Word—even the Word of a little, naked, hairless Manling—is the Word. What is in thy stomach to do when the dhole come?"

"They must swim the Waingunga. I thought to meet them with my knife in the shallows, the Pack behind me; and so stabbing and thrusting, might turn them downstream, or cool their throats."

"The dhole do not turn and their throats are hot," said Kaa. "There will be neither Manling nor Wolf cub when that hunting is done, but only dry bones."

"*Alala!* If we die, we die. It will be most good hunting. I am not wise nor strong. Hast thou a better plan, Kaa?"

"By the First Egg, I am older than many trees, and I have seen all that the Jungle has done."

"But *this* is new hunting," said Mowgli. "Never before have the dhole crossed our trail."

"What is has been. What will be is no more than a forgotten year striking backward. Be still while I count those my years."

For a long hour Mowgli lay back among the coils, while Kaa, his head motionless on the ground, thought of all that he had seen and known since the day he came from the egg. The light seemed to go out of his eyes, and now and again he made little stiff passes with his head, right and left, as though he were hunting in his sleep. Mowgli dozed quietly, for he knew that there is nothing like sleep before hunting, and he was trained to take it at any hour of the day or night. Then he felt Kaa's back grow bigger and broader below him as the huge python puffed himself out, hissing with the noise of a sword drawn from a steel scabbard.

"I have seen all the dead seasons," Kaa said at last, "and the great trees and the old elephants, and the rocks that were bare and sharp-pointed ere the moss grew. Art *thou* still alive, Manling?"

"It is only a little after moonset," said Mowgli. "I do not understand—"

"*Hssh!* I am again Kaa. Now we will go to the river, and I will show thee what is to be done against the dhole."

He turned, straight as an arrow, for the main stream of the Waingunga, plunging in a little above the pool that hid the Peace Rock, Mowgli at his side.

"Nay, do not swim. I go swiftly. My back, Little Brother."

Mowgli tucked his left arm round Kaa's neck, dropped his right close to his body, and straightened his feet. Then Kaa breasted the current as he alone could, and the ripple of the checked water stood up in a frill round Mowgli's neck, and his feet were waved to and fro in the eddy under the python's lashing sides. A mile or two above the Peace Rock (the rock which in times of drought shows dry in the center of the stream) the Waingunga narrows between a gorge of marble from eighty to a hundred feet high, and the current runs like a millrace between and over all manner of ugly stones. But Mowgli did not trouble his head about the water; he was looking at the gorge on either side and sniffing uneasily, for there was a sweetish-sourish smell in the air, very like the smell of a big anthill on a hot day. Instinctively he lowered himself in the water, only raising his head to breathe from time to time, and Kaa came to anchor with a double twist of his tail round a sunken rock, holding Mowgli in the hollow of a coil, while the water raced on.

"This is the Place of Death," said the boy. "Why do we come here?"

"They sleep," said Kaa. "Hathi will not turn aside for the Striped One. Yet Hathi and the Striped One together turn aside for the dhole, and the dhole they say turn aside for nothing. And yet for whom do the Little People of the Rocks turn aside? Tell me, Master of the Jungle, who is the Master of the Jungle?"

"These," Mowgli whispered. "It is the Place of Death. Let us go."

"Nay, look well, for they are asleep. It is as it was when I was not the length of thy arm."

The split and weatherworn rocks of the gorge of the Waingunga had been used since the beginning of the Jungle by the Little People of the Rocks—the busy, furious, black wild bees of India; and, as Mowgli knew well, all trails turned off half a mile before they reached the gorge. For centuries the Little People had hived and swarmed from cleft to cleft, and swarmed again, staining the white marble with stale honey, and made their combs tall and deep in the dark of the inner caves. The length of the gorge on both sides was hung as it were with black shimmery velvet curtains, and Mowgli sank as he looked, for those were the clotted millions of the sleeping bees. As he listened he heard more than once the rustle and slide of a honey-loaded comb turning over or falling away somewhere in the dark galleries; then a booming of angry wings, and the sullen drip, drip, drip, of the wasted honey, guttering along till it lipped over some ledge in the open air and sluggishly trickled down on the twigs. There was a tiny little beach, not five feet broad, on one side of the river, and that was piled high with the rubbish of uncounted years. There were dead bees, sweepings, and stale combs, and wings of marauding moths that had strayed in after honey, all tumbled in smooth piles of the finest black dust. The mere sharp smell of it was enough to frighten anything that had no wings, and knew what the Little People were.

Kaa moved upstream again till he came to a sandy bar at the head of the gorge.

"Here is this season's kill," said he. "Look!"

On the bank lay the skeletons of a couple of young deer and a buffalo. Mowgli could see that neither wolf nor jackal had touched the bones, which were laid out naturally.

"They came beyond the line," murmured Mowgli, "and the Little People killed them. Let us go ere they wake."

"They do not wake till the dawn," said Kaa. "Now I will tell thee. Many, many Rains ago, a hunted buck came hither from the south, a Pack on his trail. Being made blind by fear, he leaped from above, the Pack running by sight, for they were hot and blind on the trail. The sun was high, and the Little People were many and very angry. Many, too, were those of the Pack who leaped into the Waingunga, but they were dead ere they took water. Those who did not leap died in the rocks above. But the buck lived."

"How?"

"Because he came first, running for his life, leaping ere the Little People were aware, and was in the river when they gathered to kill."

"The buck lived?" Mowgli repeated slowly.

"At least he did not die *then*, though none waited his coming down with a strong body to hold him safe against the water, as a certain old fat, dead, yellow Flathead would wait for a Manling."

It was a little time before the boy spoke again. "It is to pull the very whiskers of Death, but—Kaa, thou art, indeed, the wisest of all the Jungle."

"So many have said. Look now, if the dhole follow thee—"

"As surely they will follow. Ho! ho! I have many little thorns under my tongue to prick into their hides."

"If they follow thee hot and blind, looking only at thy shoulders, those who do not die up above will take water either here or lower down, for the Little People will rise up and cover them. Now the Waingunga is hungry water, and they will go down, such as live, to the shallows by the Seeonee Lairs, and there thy Pack may meet them by the throat."

"*Ahai!* There is now only the little matter of the run and the leap. I will make me known to the dholes, so that they shall follow me very closely."

"Hast thou seen the rocks above thee? From the landward side?"

"Indeed, no. That I had forgotten."

"Go look. It is all rotten ground, cut and full of holes. One of thy clumsy feet set down without seeing would end the hunt. See,

I leave thee here, and for thy sake only I will carry word to the
Pack that they may know where to look for the dhole. For myself,
I am not of one skin with *any* wolf."

When Kaa disliked an acquaintance he could be more unpleasant
than any of the Jungle People, except perhaps Bagheera. He swam
downstream, and opposite the Rock he came on Phao and Akela
listening to the night noises.

"*Hssh!* Dogs," he said cheerfully. "The dholes will come downstream. If ye be not afraid ye can kill them in the shallows."

"When come they?" said Phao. "And where is my Man-cub?"
said Akela.

"They come when they come," said Kaa. "Wait and see. As for
thy Man-cub, from whom thou has taken a Word and so laid him
open to Death, *thy* Man-cub is with *me*, and if he be not already
dead the fault is none of thine, bleached dog! Wait here for the
dhole, and be glad that the Man-cub and I strike on thy side."

Kaa flashed upstream again, and moored himself in the middle
of the gorge, looking upward at the line of the cliff. Presently he
saw Mowgli's head move against the stars, and then there was a
whiz in the air, the keen, clean *schloop* of a body falling feet first,
and the next minute the boy was at rest again in the loop of
Kaa's body.

"It is no leap by night," said Mowgli quietly. "I have jumped
twice as far for sport; but that is an evil place above—bushes and
deep gullies, all full of the Little People. I have put big stones one
above the other by the side of three gullies. These I shall throw
down with my feet in running, and the Little People will rise up
behind me, very angry."

"That is Man's talk and Man's cunning," said Kaa. "Thou art
wise, but the Little People are always angry."

"Nay, at twilight all wings near and far rest for a while. I will
play with the dhole at twilight, for the dhole hunts best by day.
He follows now Won-tolla's blood trail."

"Chil does not leave a dead ox, nor the dhole the blood trail,"
said Kaa.

"Then I will make him a new blood trail, of his own blood, if

I can. Thou wilt stay here, Kaa, till I come again with my dholes?"

"Ay, but what if they kill thee in the Jungle, or the Little People kill thee before thou canst leap down to the river?"

"When I am dead it is time to sing the Death Song," said Mowgli, quoting a Jungle saying. "Good hunting, Kaa!"

He loosed his arm from the python's neck and, laughing aloud from sheer happiness, paddled down the gorge toward the far bank, where he found slack water. There was nothing Mowgli liked better than "to pull the whiskers of Death," and make the Jungle know that he was their overlord. He had often, with Baloo's help, robbed bees' nests in single trees, and he knew that the Little People hated the smell of wild garlic. So he gathered a small bundle of it, tied it up with a bark string, and then followed Won-tolla's blood trail, as it ran southerly from the Lairs, for some five miles, looking at the trees with his head on one side, and chuckling as he looked.

"Mowgli, the Frog, have I been," said he to himself; "Mowgli, the Wolf, have I said that I am. Now Mowgli, the Ape, must I be before I am Mowgli, the Buck. At the end I shall be Mowgli, the Man. Ho!" and he slid his thumb along the blade of his knife.

Won-tolla's trail, all rank with dark blood spots, ran back under a forest of thick trees that stretched away northeastward, gradually growing thinner and thinner to within two miles of the Bee Rocks. From the last tree to the low scrub of the Bee Rocks was open country. Mowgli trotted along under the trees, judging distances between branch and branch, occasionally climbing up a trunk and taking a trial leap from one tree to another till he came to the open ground, which he studied very carefully for an hour. Then he turned, picked up Won-tolla's trail where he had left it, settled himself in a tree with an outrunning branch some eight feet from the ground, and sat still, sharpening his knife on the sole of his foot and singing to himself.

A little before midday, when the sun was very warm, he heard the patter of feet and smelled the abominable smell of the dhole pack as they trotted pitilessly along Won-tolla's trail. Seen from above, the red dhole does not look half the size of a wolf, but

Mowgli knew how strong his feet and jaws were. He watched the sharp bay head of the leader snuffing along the trail, and gave him "Good hunting!"

The brute looked up, and his companions halted behind him, scores and scores of red dogs with low-hung tails, heavy shoulders, weak quarters, and bloody mouths. The dholes are a very silent people as a rule, and they have no manners even in their own Jungle. Fully two hundred must have gathered below him, but he could see that the leaders sniffed hungrily on Won-tolla's trail, and tried to drag the Pack forward. That would never do, or they would be at the Lairs in broad daylight, and Mowgli meant to hold them under his tree till dusk.

"By whose leave do ye come here?" said Mowgli.

"All Jungles are our Jungle," was the reply, and the dhole that gave it bared his white teeth. Mowgli looked down with a smile, and imitated perfectly the sharp chitter-chatter of Chikai, the leaping rat of the Deccan, meaning the dholes to understand that he considered them no better than Chikai. The Pack closed up round the tree trunk and the leader bayed savagely, calling Mowgli a tree ape. For an answer Mowgli stretched down one naked leg and wriggled his bare toes just above the leader's head. That was enough to wake the Pack to stupid rage. Mowgli caught his foot away as the leader leaped up, and said sweetly: "Dog, red dog! Go back to the Deccan and eat lizards. Go to Chikai thy brother—red, red dog! There is hair between every toe!"

"Come down ere we starve thee out, hairless ape!" yelled the Pack, and this was exactly what Mowgli wanted. He laid himself down along the branch, his cheek to the bark, his right arm free, and there he told the Pack what he thought about them, their manners, their customs, their mates, and their puppies. There is no speech in the world so rancorous and so stinging as the language the Jungle People use to show scorn and contempt. As Mowgli told Kaa, he had many little thorns under his tongue, and slowly and deliberately he drove the dholes from silence to growls, from growls to yells, and from yells to hoarse ravings. All the while Mowgli's right hand lay crooked at his side, ready for action, his feet locked round the branch. The big bay leader had leaped many times in the air, but Mowgli dared not risk a false blow. At last, made furious beyond his natural strength, he bounded up seven or eight feet clear of the ground. Then Mowgli's hand shot out like the head of a tree snake, and gripped him by the scruff of his neck, and the branch shook with the jar as his weight fell back, almost wrenching Mowgli to the ground. But he never loosed his grip, and inch by inch he hauled the beast up on the branch. With his left hand he reached for his knife and cut off the red, bushy tail, flinging the dhole back to earth again. That was all he needed. The Pack would not go forward on Won-tolla's trail now till they had killed Mowgli or Mowgli had killed them. He saw them settle down in circles with a quiver of the haunches that meant they were going to stay, and so he climbed to a higher crotch, settled his back comfortably, and went to sleep.

After three or four hours he waked and counted the Pack. They were all there, silent, husky, and dry, with eyes of steel. The sun was beginning to sink. In half an hour the Little People of the Rocks would be ending their labors, and, as you know, the dhole does not fight best in the twilight. "I did not need such faithful watchers," he said politely, standing up on a branch, "but I will remember this. Ye be true dholes, but to my thinking overmuch of one kind. For that reason I do not give the big lizard-eater his tail again. Art thou not pleased, Red Dog?"

"I myself will tear out thy stomach!" yelled the leader, scratching at the foot of the tree.

"Nay, but consider, wise rat of the Deccan. There will now be many litters of little tailless red dogs, yea, with raw red stumps that sting when the sand is hot. Go home, Red Dog, and cry that an ape has done this. Ye will not go? Come, then, with me, and I will make you very wise!"

He moved, Bandar-log fashion, into the next tree, and so on into the next and the next, the Pack, with their red coats all aflame, huddling and following below. Now and then he would pretend to fall, and the Pack would tumble one over the other in their haste to be at the death. When Mowgli came to the last tree he took the garlic and rubbed himself all over carefully, and the dholes yelled with scorn. "Ape with a wolf's tongue, dost thou think to cover thy scent?" they said. "We follow to the death."

"Take thy tail," said Mowgli, flinging it back along the course he had taken. The Pack instinctively rushed after it. "And follow now—to the death."

He had slipped down the tree trunk, and headed like the wind in bare feet for the Bee Rocks, before the dholes saw what he would do.

They gave one deep howl, and settled down to the long canter that can at the last run down anything that runs. Mowgli knew their pack-pace to be much slower than that of the wolves, or he would never have risked a two-mile run in full sight. He ran cleanly, evenly, and springily; the tailless leader not five yards behind him; and the Pack tailing out over perhaps a quarter of a mile of ground, crazy and blind with the rage of slaughter. So he kept his distance by ear, reserving his last effort for the rush across the Bee Rocks.

The Little People had gone to sleep in the early twilight; but as Mowgli's first footfalls rang on the hollow ground he heard a sound as though all the earth were humming. Then he ran as he had never run in his life before, spurned aside one—two—three of the piles of stones into the dark, sweet-smelling gullies; heard a roar like the roar of the sea in a cave; saw with the tail of his eye the air grow dark behind him; saw the current of the Waingunga far below, and a flat, diamond-shaped head in the water; leaped outward with all his strength, the tailless dhole snapping at his shoulder in midair, and dropped feet first to the safety of the river, breathless and triumphant. There was not a sting upon him, for the smell of the garlic had checked the Little People for just the few seconds that he was among them. When he rose Kaa's coils were steadying him and things were bounding over the edge of the cliff—great lumps, it seemed, of clustered bees falling like plummets; but before any lump touched water the bees flew upward and the body of a dhole whirled downstream. Overhead they could hear furious short yells that were drowned in a roar like breakers—the roar of the wings of the Little People of the Rocks. Some of the dholes had leaped short into the trees on the cliffs, and the bees blotted out their shapes; but the greater number of them, maddened by the stings, had flung themselves into the river; and, as Kaa said, the Waingunga was hungry water.

Kaa held Mowgli fast till the boy had recovered his breath. "We may not stay here," he said. "The Little People are roused indeed. Come!"

Swimming low and diving as often as he could, Mowgli went down the river, knife in hand.

"Slowly, slowly," said Kaa. "Many of the dholes took water swiftly when they saw the Little People rise."

"The more work for my knife, then. *Phai!* How the Little People follow!" Mowgli sank again. The face of the water was blanketed with wild bees, buzzing, and stinging all they found.

"Nothing was ever yet lost by silence," said Kaa—no sting could penetrate his scales—"and thou hast all the long night for the hunting. Hear them howl!"

Nearly half the pack had seen the trap their fellows rushed into, and turning sharp aside had flung themselves into the water where the gorge broke down in steep banks. To remain ashore was death, and every dhole knew it. Their pack was swept along the current, down to the deep eddies of the Peace Pool, but even there the angry Little People followed and forced them to the water again. Mowgli could hear the voice of the tailless leader bidding his people hold on and kill every wolf in Seeonee. But he did not waste his time in listening.

"One kills in the dark behind us!" snapped a dhole. "Here is tainted water!"

Mowgli had dived forward like an otter, twitched a struggling dhole under water before he could open his mouth, and dark rings rose as the body plopped up, turning on its side. The dholes tried to turn, but the current prevented them, and the Little People darted at the heads and ears, and they could hear the challenge of the Seeonee Pack growing louder and deeper in the gathering darkness. Again Mowgli dived, and again a dhole went under, and rose dead, and again the clamor broke out at the rear of the pack; some howling that it was best to go ashore, others calling on their leader to lead them back to the Deccan, and others bidding Mowgli show himself and be killed.

"They come to the fight with two stomachs and several voices," said Kaa. "The rest is with thy brethren below yonder. The Little People go back to sleep. They have chased us far. Now I, too, turn back, for I am not of one skin with any wolf. Good hunting, Little Brother, and remember the dhole bites low."

A wolf came running along the bank on three legs, leaping up and down, laying his head sideways close to the ground, hunching his back, and breaking high into the air, as though he were playing with his cubs. It was Won-tolla, the Outlier, and he said never a word, but continued his horrible sport beside the dholes. They had been long in the water now, and were swimming wearily, their bushy tails dragging like sponges, so tired and shaken that they, too, were silent, watching the pair of blazing eyes that moved abreast.

"Art thou there, Man-cub?" said Won-tolla across the water.

"Ask of the dead, Outlier," Mowgli replied. "Have none come downstream? I have filled these dogs' mouths with dirt; I have tricked them in the broad daylight, and their leader lacks his tail, but here be some few for thee still. Whither shall I drive them?"

"I will wait," said Won-tolla. "The night is before me."

Nearer and nearer came the bay of the Seeonee wolves. "For the Pack, for the Full Pack it is met!" and a bend in the river drove the dholes forward among the sands and shoals opposite the Lairs.

The bank was lined with burning eyes, and except for the horrible *pheeal* that had never stopped since sundown, there was no sound in the Jungle. It seemed as though Won-tolla were fawning on them to come ashore; and "Turn and take hold!" said the leader of the dholes. The entire Pack flung themselves at the shore, threshing through the shoal water, till the face of the Waingunga was all white and torn, and great ripples went from side to side. Mowgli followed the rush, stabbing and slicing as the dholes, huddled together, rushed up the river beach in one wave.

Then the long fight began, heaving and straining and splitting and scattering along the red, wet sands, and over and between the tangled tree roots, and through and among the bushes; for even now the dholes were two to one. But they met wolves fighting for all that made the Pack, and not only the short, high, deep-chested, white-tusked hunters of the Pack, but the anxious-eyed lahinis— the she-wolves of the lair—fighting for their litters, with here and there a yearling wolf, his first coat still half woolly, tugging and grappling by their sides.

A wolf flies at the throat or snaps at the flank, while a dhole, by preference, bites at the belly; so when the dholes were struggling out of the water and had to raise their heads, the odds were with the wolves. On dry land the wolves suffered; but in the water or ashore, Mowgli's knife came and went without ceasing. The Four had worried their way to his side. Gray Brother, crouched between the boy's knees, was protecting his stomach, while the others guarded his back and either side, or stood over him when the shock of a leaping, yelling dhole who had thrown himself full on the steady blade bore him down. For the rest, it was one tangled confusion—a locked and swaying mob that moved from right to left and from left to right along the bank. Here would be a heaving mound, like a water blister in a whirlpool, which would break like a water blister, and throw up four or five mangled dogs; here a yearling cub would be held up by the pressure round him, though he had been killed early, while his mother, crazed with dumb rage, rolled over and over, snapping; and in the middle of the thickest press, perhaps, one wolf and one dhole, forgetting everything else, would be maneuvering for first hold till they were whirled away by a rush of furious fighters. Once Mowgli passed Akela, a dhole on either flank, and his all but toothless jaws closed over the loins of a third; and once he saw Phao, his teeth set in the throat of a dhole, tugging the unwilling beast forward till the yearlings could finish him. As the night wore on, the quick, giddy-go-round motion increased. The dholes were cowed and afraid to attack the stronger wolves, but did not yet dare to run away. Mowgli felt that the end was coming soon, and contented himself with striking merely to cripple. There was time now and again to breathe, and pass a word to a friend, and the mere flicker of the knife would sometimes turn a dog aside.

"The meat is very near the bone," Gray Brother yelled. He was bleeding from a score of flesh wounds.

"But the bone is yet to be cracked," said Mowgli. "*Eowawa! Thus* do we do in the Jungle!" The red blade ran like a flame along the side of a dhole whose hindquarters were hidden by the weight of a clinging wolf.

"My kill!" snorted the wolf. "Leave him to me."

"Is thy stomach still empty, Outlier?" said Mowgli. Won-tolla was fearfully punished, but his grip had paralyzed the dhole, who could not turn round and reach him.

"By the Bull that bought me," said Mowgli, with a bitter laugh, "it is the tailless one!" And indeed it was the big bay-colored leader.

"It is not wise to kill cubs and lahinis," Mowgli went on philosophically, wiping the blood out of his eyes, "unless one has also killed the Outlier; and it is in my stomach that this Won-tolla kills thee."

A dhole leaped to his leader's aid; but before his teeth had found Won-tolla's flank, Mowgli's knife was in his throat, and Gray Brother took what was left.

"And thus do we do in the Jungle," said Mowgli.

Won-tolla said not a word, only his jaws were closing and closing on the backbone as his life ebbed. The dhole shuddered, his head dropped, and he lay still, and Won-tolla dropped above him.

"*Huh!* The Blood Debt is paid," said Mowgli. "Sing the song, Won-tolla."

"He hunts no more," said Gray Brother; "and Akela, too, is silent this long time."

"The bone is cracked!" thundered Phao, son of Phaona. "They go! Kill, kill out, O hunters of the Free People!"

Dhole after dhole was slinking away from those dark and bloody sands to the river, to the thick Jungle, upstream or downstream as he saw the road clear.

"The debt! Pay the debt!" shouted Mowgli. "They have slain the Lone Wolf! Let not a dog go!"

He was flying to the river, knife in hand, to check any dhole who dared to take water, when, from under a mound of nine dead, rose Akela's head and forequarters, and Mowgli dropped on his knees beside the Lone Wolf.

"Said I not it would be my last fight?" Akela gasped. "It is good hunting. And thou, Little Brother?"

"I live, having killed many."

"Even so. I die, and I would—I would die by thee, Little Brother." Mowgli took the scarred head on his knees, and put his arms round the torn neck. "It is long since the old days of Shere Khan, and a Man-cub that rolled naked in the dust."

"Nay, nay, I am a wolf. I am of one skin with the Free People," Mowgli cried. "It is no will of mine that I am a man."

"Thou art a man, Little Brother. Thou art a man, or else the Pack had fled before the dhole. My life I owe to thee, and today thou hast saved the Pack even as once I saved thee. Hast thou forgotten? All debts are paid now. Go to thine own people. I tell thee again, eye of my eye, this hunting is ended. Go to thine own people."

"I will never go. I will hunt alone in the Jungle."

"After the summer come the Rains, and after the Rains comes the spring. Go back before thou art driven."

"Who will drive me?"

"Mowgli will drive Mowgli. Go back to thy people."

"When Mowgli drives Mowgli I will go," Mowgli answered.

"There is no more to say," said Akela. "Little Brother, canst thou raise me to my feet? I also was a leader of the Free People."

Very carefully and gently Mowgli raised Akela to his feet, both arms round him, and the Lone Wolf drew a long breath, and began the Death Song that a leader of the Pack should sing when he dies. It gathered strength as he went on, ringing far across the river, till it came to the last "Good hunting!" and Akela shook himself clear of Mowgli for an instant, and, leaping into the air, fell backward dead upon his last and most terrible kill.

Mowgli sat with his head on his knees, careless of anything else, while the remnant of the flying dholes were being run down by the merciless lahinis. Little by little the cries died away, and the wolves returned limping, to take stock of the losses. Fifteen of the Pack, as well as half a dozen lahinis, lay dead by the river, and of the others not one was unmarked. And Mowgli sat till daybreak, when Phao's wet, red muzzle was dropped in his hand, and Mowgli drew back to show the gaunt body of Akela.

"Good hunting!" said Phao, as though Akela were still alive, and then over his bitten shoulder to the others: "Howl, dogs! A Wolf has died tonight!"

But of all the Pack of two hundred fighting dholes, whose boast was that all Jungles were their Jungle, not one returned to the Deccan to carry that word.

THE SECOND YEAR after the great fight with Red Dog and the death of Akela, Mowgli must have been nearly seventeen years old. He looked older, for hard exercise and the best of good eating had given him strength and growth far beyond his age. He could swing by one hand from a top branch for half an hour at a time, when he had occasion to look along the tree roads. He could stop a young buck in mid-gallop and throw him sideways by the head. The Jungle People who used to fear him for his wits feared him now for his strength, and when he moved quietly on his own affairs the mere whisper of his coming cleared the wood paths. And yet the look in his eyes was always gentle. Even when he fought, his eyes never blazed as Bagheera's did; that was one of the things that Bagheera himself did not understand.

He asked Mowgli about it, and the boy laughed and said: "When I miss the kill I am angry. When I must go empty for two days I am very angry. Do not my eyes talk then?"

"The mouth is hungry," said Bagheera, "but the eyes say nothing. Hunting, eating, or swimming, it is all one—like a stone in wet or dry weather." Mowgli looked at him lazily from under his long eyelashes, and, as usual, the panther's head dropped. Bagheera knew his master.

They were lying out far up the side of a hill overlooking the Waingunga, and the morning mists hung below them in bands of white and green. As the sun rose it changed into bubbling seas of red gold and let the low rays stripe the dried grass on which Mowgli and Bagheera were resting. It was the end of the cold weather, the leaves and the trees looked worn and faded, and there was a dry, ticking rustle everywhere when the wind blew.

"The year turns," Bagheera said. "The Jungle goes forward. The Time of New Talk is near. It is very good."

"The grass is dry," Mowgli answered, pulling up a tuft. "Even Eye-of-the-Spring [that is a little trumpet-shaped, waxy red flower that runs in and out among the grasses] is shut, and . . . Bagheera, *is* it well for the Black Panther so to lie on his back and beat with his paws in the air, as though he were the tree cat?"

"Aowh?" said Bagheera. He seemed to be thinking of other things.

"I say, *is* it well for the Black Panther so to mouth and cough, and howl and roll? Remember, we be the Masters of the Jungle, thou and I."

"Indeed, yes; I hear, Man-cub." Bagheera rolled over hurriedly and sat up, the dust on his ragged black flanks. (He was just casting his winter coat.) "We be surely the Masters of the Jungle! Who is so strong as Mowgli? Who so wise?" There was a curious drawl in the voice that made Mowgli turn to see whether by any chance the Black Panther were making fun of him, for the Jungle is full of words that sound like one thing, but mean another.

Mowgli sat with his elbows on his knees, looking out across the valley at the daylight. Somewhere down in the woods below a bird was trying over in a husky, reedy voice the first few notes of his spring song.

"I said the Time of New Talk is near," growled the panther,

switching his tail. "That is Ferao, the scarlet woodpecker. *He* has not forgotten. Now I, too, must remember my song," and he began purring and crooning to himself.

"There is no game afoot," said Mowgli.

"Little Brother, are *both* thine ears stopped? That is no killing word, but my song that I make ready against the need."

"I had forgotten. I shall know when the Time of New Talk is here, because then thou and the others all run away and leave me alone." Mowgli spoke rather savagely. "How was it last season, when I would gather sugarcane from the fields of a Man Pack? I sent a runner—I sent thee!—to Hathi, bidding him to come upon such a night and pluck the sweet grass for me with his trunk."

"He came only two nights later," said Bagheera, cowering a little; "and of that long, sweet grass that pleased thee so he gathered more than any Man-cub could eat in all the nights of the Rains. That was no fault of mine."

"He did not come upon the night when I sent him the word. No, he was trumpeting and running and roaring through the valleys in the moonlight, his trail like the trail of three elephants. He danced in the moonlight before the houses of the Man Pack. I saw him, and yet he would not come to me; and *I* am the Master of the Jungle!"

"It was the Time of New Talk," said the panther. "Perhaps, Little Brother, thou didst not that time call him by a Master Word? Listen to Ferao, and be glad!"

Mowgli's bad temper seemed to have boiled itself away. He lay back with his head on his arms, his eyes shut. "I do not know— nor do I care," he said sleepily. "Let us sleep, Bagheera. My stomach is heavy in me. Make me a rest for my head."

In an Indian Jungle the seasons slide one into the other almost without division. There seem to be only two—the wet and the dry; but if you look closely below the torrents of rain and the clouds of dust you will find all four going round in their regular ring. Spring is the most wonderful, because she has not to cover a clean, bare field with new leaves and flowers, but to drive before her and to put away the oversurviving raffle of half-green things which the gentle winter has suffered to live, and to make the stale earth feel new and young once more. And this she does so well that there is no spring in the world like the Jungle spring.

There is one day when all things are tired, and the very smells, as they drift on the heavy air, are old and used. Then there is another day—to the eye nothing whatever has changed—when all the smells are new and delightful, and the whiskers of the Jungle People quiver to their roots, and the winter hair comes away from their sides in long, draggled locks. Then, perhaps, a little rain falls, and all the trees and the bamboos and the mosses and the juicy-leaved plants wake with a noise of growing that you can almost hear, and under this noise runs, day and night, a deep hum. *That* is the noise of spring—the purring of the warm, happy world.

Up to this year Mowgli had always delighted in the turn of the seasons. In the spring his voice could be heard in all sorts of wet, starlighted, blossoming places, helping the big frogs through their choruses, or mocking the little upside-down owls that hoot through the white nights. Like all his people, spring was the season he chose for his flittings—moving, for the mere joy of rushing through the warm air, thirty, forty, or fifty miles between twilight and the morning star, and coming back panting and laughing and wreathed with strange flowers.

But that spring, as he told Bagheera, his stomach was changed in him. Ever since the bamboo shoots turned spotty brown he had been looking forward to the morning when the smells should change. But when the morning came, and Mor, the Peacock, blazing in bronze and blue and gold, cried it aloud all along the misty woods, and Mowgli opened his mouth to send on the cry, the words choked between his teeth, and a feeling came over him that began at his toes and ended in his hair—a feeling of pure unhappiness, so that he looked himself over to be sure that he had not trod on a thorn. Mor cried the new smells, the other birds took it over, and from the rocks by the Waingunga he heard Bagheera's hoarse scream—something between the scream of an eagle and the neighing of a horse. There was a yelling and scattering of

Bandar-log in the new-budding branches above, and there stood Mowgli, his chest, filled to answer Mor, sinking in little gasps as the breath was driven out of it by this unhappiness.

He stared all round him, but he could see no more than the mocking Bandar-log scudding through the trees, and Mor, his tail spread in full splendor, dancing on the slopes below.

"The smells have changed," screamed Mor. "Good hunting, Little Brother! Where is thy answer?"

"Little Brother, good hunting!" whistled Chil, the Kite, and his mate, swooping down together. The two swooped under Mowgli's nose so close that a pinch of downy white feathers brushed away.

A light spring rain drove across the Jungle in a belt half a mile wide, left the new leaves wet and nodding behind, and died out in a double rainbow and a light roll of thunder. The spring hum broke out for a minute, and was silent, but all the Jungle Folk seemed to be giving tongue at once. All except Mowgli.

"I have eaten good food," he said to himself. "I have drunk good water. But my stomach is heavy, and I have given very bad talk to the people of the Jungle. Now, too, I am hot and now I am cold, and now I am neither hot nor cold, but angry with that which I cannot see. Huhu! It is time to make a running! Tonight I will make a spring running to the Marshes of the North, and back again. I have hunted too easily too long. The Four shall come with me, for they grow as fat as white grubs."

He called, but never one of the Four answered. They were far beyond earshot, singing over the spring songs with the wolves of the Pack. He gave the sharp, barking note, but his only answer was the mocking *miaou* of the little spotted tree cat winding in and out among the branches for early birds' nests. At this he shook all over with rage, and half drew his knife. Then he became very haughty, though there was no one to see him, and stalked severely down the hillside, chin up and eyebrows down.

"Yes," said Mowgli to himself, though in his heart he knew that he had no reason. "Let the Red Dhole come from the Deccan, and all the Jungle runs whining to Mowgli, calling him great elephant names. But now, because Eye-of-the-Spring is red, and Mor, forsooth, must show his naked legs in some spring dance, the Jungle goes mad as Tabaqui. . . . By the Bull that bought me! Am I the Master of the Jungle, or am I not? Be silent! What do ye here?"

A couple of young wolves of the Pack were cantering down a path, looking for open ground in which to fight. Their neck bristles were as stiff as wire, and they bayed furiously, crouching for the first grapple. Mowgli leaped forward, caught one out-stretched throat in either hand, expecting to fling the creatures backward as he had often done in games or Pack hunts. But he had never before interfered with a spring fight. The two leaped forward and dashed him aside, and without word to waste rolled over and over close-locked.

Mowgli was on his feet almost before he fell, his knife and his white teeth bared, and at that minute he would have killed both for no reason but that they were fighting when he wished them to be quiet. He danced round them with lowered shoulders and quivering hand, ready to send in a double blow when the first flurry of the scuffle should be over; but while he waited the strength seemed to ebb from his body, the knife point lowered, and he sheathed the knife and watched.

"I have surely eaten poison," he sighed at last. "Since I broke up the Council with the Red Flower—since I killed Shere Khan—none of the Pack could fling me aside. My strength is gone from me, and presently I shall die. Oh, Mowgli, why dost thou not kill them both?"

The fight went on till one wolf ran away, and Mowgli was left alone on the torn and bloody ground, while the feeling of unhappiness he had never known before covered him as water covers a log.

He killed early that evening and ate but little, so as to be in good fettle for his spring running, and he ate alone because all the Jungle People were away singing or fighting. It was a perfect white night, as they call it. All green things seemed to have made a month's growth since the morning. The mosses curled deep and warm over his feet, the young grass had no cutting edges, and all the voices of the Jungle boomed like one deep harp string touched by the moon—the Moon of New Talk, who splashed her light full on rock and pool, slipped it between trunk and creeper, and sifted it through a million leaves. Forgetting his unhappiness, Mowgli sang aloud with pure delight as he settled into his stride. It was more like flying than anything else, for he had chosen the long downward slope that leads to the Northern Marshes through the heart of the main Jungle, where the springy ground deadened the fall of his feet. When he tired of ground-going he threw up his hands monkey fashion to the nearest creeper, and seemed to float rather than to climb up into the thin branches, whence he would follow a tree road till his mood changed, and he shot downward in a long, leafy curve to the levels again. There were thickets where the wet young growth stood breast-high about him; and hilltops crowned with broken rock, where he leaped from stone to stone above the lairs of the frightened little foxes. He would hear, very faint and far off, the *chug-drug* of a boar sharpening his tusks on a bole; and would come across the great gray brute all alone, scribing and rending the bark of a tall tree, his mouth dripping with foam, and his eyes blazing like fire. Or he would turn aside to the sound of clashing horns and hissing grunts, and dash past a couple of furious sambars, staggering to and fro with lowered heads, striped with blood that showed black in the moonlight.

So he ran, sometimes shouting, sometimes singing to himself, the happiest thing in all the Jungle that night, till the smell of the flowers warned him that he was near the marshes, and those lay far beyond his farthest hunting grounds.

Here a man-trained man would have sunk overhead in three strides, but Mowgli's feet had eyes in them, and they passed him from tussock to tussock and clump to quaking clump without asking help from the eyes in his head. He ran out to the middle of the swamp, disturbing the duck as he ran, and sat down on a moss-coated tree trunk lapped in the black water. The marsh was awake all round him, for in the spring the Bird People sleep very lightly, and companies of them were coming or going the night through. But no one took any notice of Mowgli sitting among the tall reeds humming songs without words, and looking at the soles of his hard brown feet in case of neglected thorns. All his unhappiness seemed to have been left behind in his own Jungle, and he was just beginning a full-throat song when it came back again—ten times worse than before.

This time Mowgli was frightened. "It is here also!" he said half aloud. "It has followed me," and he looked over his shoulder to see whether the It were not standing behind him. "There is no one here." The night noises of the marsh went on, but never a bird or beast spoke to him, and the new feeling of misery grew.

"I have surely eaten poison," he said in an awestricken voice. "My strength is going from me. I was afraid—and yet it was not *I* that was afraid—Mowgli was afraid when the two wolves fought. Akela, or even Phao, would have silenced them; yet Mowgli was afraid. That is true sign I have eaten poison. . . . But what do they care in the Jungle?"

He was so sorry for himself that he nearly wept. "And after," he went on, "they will find me lying in the black water. Nay, I will go back to my own Jungle, and I will die upon the Council Rock, and Bagheera, perhaps, may watch by what is left for a little, lest Chil use me as he used Akela."

A large, warm tear splashed down on his knee, and, miserable as he was, Mowgli felt happy that he was so miserable, if you can understand that upside-down sort of happiness. "As Chil, the Kite, used Akela," he repeated, "on the night I saved the Pack from Red Dog." He was quiet for a little, thinking of the last words of the Lone Wolf. "Now Akela said to me many foolish things before he died, for when we die our stomachs change. He said . . . None the less, I *am* of the Jungle!"

In his excitement, as he remembered the fight on Waingunga bank, he shouted the last words, and a wild buffalo-cow among the reeds sprang to her knees, snorting, "Man!"

"Uhh!" said Mysa, the Wild Buffalo (Mowgli could hear him turn in his wallow), "*that* is no man. It is only the hairless wolf of the Seeonee Pack. On such nights runs he to and fro."

Mowgli could not resist the temptation of stealing across the reeds to Mysa and pricking him with the point of his knife. The great dripping bull broke out of his wallow like a shell exploding, while Mowgli laughed till he sat down.

"Say now that the hairless wolf of the Seeonee Pack once herded thee, Mysa," he called.

"Wolf! *Thou?*" the bull snorted, stamping in the mud. "All the Jungle knows thou wast a herder of tame cattle—such a man's brat as shouts in the dust by the crops yonder. *Thou* of the Jungle! Come to firm ground and I will . . ." Mysa frothed at the mouth, for Mysa has nearly the worst temper of anyone in the Jungle.

Mowgli watched him puff and blow with eyes that never changed. When he could make himself heard through the pattering mud, he said: "What Man Pack lair here by the marshes, Mysa? This is new Jungle to me."

"Go north, then," roared the angry bull, for Mowgli had pricked him rather sharply. "Go and tell them at the village at the foot of the marsh."

"I will go and look at this village. Softly now. It is not every night that the Master of the Jungle comes to herd thee."

He stepped out to the shivering ground on the edge of the marsh, well knowing that Mysa would never charge over it, and laughed, as he ran, to think of the bull's anger.

"My strength is not altogether gone," he said. "It may be that the poison is not to the bone. There is a star sitting low yonder." He looked at it between his half-shut hands. "By the Bull that bought me, it is the Red Flower—the Red Flower that I lay beside before I came even to the first Seeonee Pack! Now that I have seen, I will finish the running."

The marsh ended in a broad plain where a light twinkled. It was a long time since Mowgli had concerned himself with the doings of men, but this night the glimmer of the Red Flower drew him forward. Forgetting that he was no longer in his own Jungle, where he could do what he pleased, he trod carelessly through the dew-loaded grasses till he came to the hut where the light stood. Three or four yelping dogs gave tongue, for he was on the outskirts of a village.

"Ho!" said Mowgli, sitting down noiselessly, after sending back a deep wolf growl that silenced the curs. "What comes will come. Mowgli, what hast thou to do anymore with the lairs of the Man Pack?" He rubbed his mouth, remembering where a stone had struck it years ago when the other Man Pack had cast him out.

The door of the hut opened, and a woman stood peering out into the darkness. A child cried, and the woman said over her shoulder, "Sleep. It was but a jackal that waked the dogs. In a little time morning comes."

Mowgli in the grass began to shake as though he had fever. He knew that voice well, but to make sure he cried softly, surprised to find how man's talk came back, "Messua! O Messua!"

"Who calls?" said the woman, a quiver in her voice.

"Hast thou forgotten?" said Mowgli. His throat was dry as he spoke.

"If it be *thou*, what name did I give thee? Say!" She had half shut the door, and her hand was clutching at her breast.

"Nathoo! Ohé, Nathoo!" said Mowgli, for that was the name Messua gave him when he first came to the Man Pack.

"Come, my son," she called, and Mowgli stepped into the light, and looked full at Messua, the woman who had been good to him. She was older, and her hair was gray, but her eyes and her voice had not changed. Womanlike, she expected to find Mowgli where she had left him, and her eyes traveled upward in a puzzled way from his chest to his head that touched the top of the door.

"My son," she stammered; and then, sinking to his feet: "But it is no longer my son. It is a Godling of the Woods! Ahai!"

As he stood in the red light of the oil lamp, strong, tall, and beautiful, his long black hair sweeping over his shoulders, his head crowned with a wreath of white jasmine, he might easily have been mistaken for some wild god of a Jungle legend. The child half asleep on a cot sprang up and shrieked aloud with terror. Messua turned to soothe him, while Mowgli stood still, looking in at the water jars and the cooking pots, the grain bin, and all the other human belongings that he found himself remembering so well.

"What wilt thou eat or drink?" Messua murmured. "This is all thine. But art thou him I called Nathoo, or a Godling, indeed?"

"I am Nathoo," said Mowgli. "I am very far from my own place. I saw this light, and came hither. I did not know thou wast here."

"After you went back to the Jungle," Messua said timidly, "the village would have burned us to death, for the people said we were the father and mother of a Devil Child. We escaped and came to this village, and my man took service in the fields. At last—for, indeed, he was a strong man—we held a little land here. It is not so rich as the old village, but we do not need much."

"Where is the man?"

"He is dead—a year."

"And he?" Mowgli pointed to the child.

"My son that was born two Rains ago. If thou art a Godling, give him the Favor of the Jungle, that he may be safe among thy— thy people." She lifted up the child, who, forgetting his fright, reached out to play with the knife that hung on Mowgli's chest, and Mowgli put the little fingers aside very carefully.

"And if thou art Nathoo whom the tiger carried away," Messua went on, choking, "he is then thy younger brother. Give him an elder brother's blessing."

"*Hai-mai!* What do I know of the thing called a blessing? I am neither a Godling nor his brother, and— O mother, mother, my heart is heavy in me." He shivered as he set down the child.

"Like enough," said Messua, bustling among the cooking pots, "this comes of running about the marshes by night. Beyond question, the fever had soaked thee to the marrow." Mowgli smiled a little at the idea of anything in the Jungle hurting him. "I will make a fire, and thou shalt drink warm milk. Put away the jasmine wreath: the smell is heavy in so small a place."

Mowgli sat down, muttering, with his face in his hands. All manner of strange feelings that he had never felt before were running over him, and he felt dizzy and a little sick. He drank the warm milk in long gulps, Messua patting him on the shoulder from time to time.

"Son," she said at last—her eyes were full of pride—"have any told thee that thou art beautiful beyond all men?"

"Hah?" said Mowgli, for naturally he had never heard anything of the kind. Messua laughed softly and happily. The look in his face was enough for her.

"I am the first, then? It is right, though it comes seldom, that a mother should tell her son these good things. Thou art very beautiful. Never have I looked upon such a man."

Mowgli twisted his head and tried to see over his own hard shoulder, and Messua laughed again so long that Mowgli, not knowing why, was forced to laugh with her, and the child ran from one to the other, laughing too.

"Nay, thou must not mock thy brother," said Messua, catching him to her breast. "When thou art one half as fair we will marry thee to the youngest daughter of a king, and thou shalt ride great elephants."

Mowgli could not understand one word in three of the talk here; the warm milk was taking effect on him after his long run, so he curled up and in a minute was deep asleep, and Messua put the hair back from his eyes, threw a cloth over him, and was happy. Jungle fashion, he slept out the rest of that night and all the next day; for his instincts, which never wholly slept, warned him there was nothing to fear. He waked at last with a bound that shook the hut, for the cloth over his face made him dream of traps; and there he stood, his hand on his knife, the sleep all heavy in his rolling eyes, ready for any fight.

Messua laughed, and set the evening meal before him. There were only a few coarse cakes baked over the smoky fire, some rice, and a lump of sour preserved tamarinds—just enough to go on with till he could get to his evening kill. The smell of the dew in the marshes made him hungry and restless. He wanted to finish his spring running, but the child insisted on sitting in his arms, and Messua would have it that his long, blue-black hair must be combed out. So she sang, as she combed, foolish little baby songs, now calling Mowgli her son, and now begging him to give some of his Jungle power to the child. The hut door was closed, but Mowgli heard a sound he knew well, and saw Messua's jaw drop with horror as a great gray paw came under the bottom of the door, and Gray Brother outside whined a muffled and penitent whine of anxiety and fear.

"Out and wait! Ye would not come when I called," said Mowgli in Jungle talk, without turning his head, and the great gray paw disappeared.

"Do not—do not bring thy—thy servants with thee," said Messua. "I—we have always lived at peace with the Jungle."

"It is peace," said Mowgli, rising. "But I see that even in spring-time the Jungle People do not always forget. Mother, I go."

Messua drew aside humbly—he was indeed a wood god, she thought; but as his hand was on the door the mother in her made her throw her arms round Mowgli's neck again and again.

"Come back!" she whispered. "Son or no son, come back, for I love thee— Look, he too grieves."

The child was crying because the man with the shiny knife was going away.

"Come back again," Messua repeated. "By night or by day this door is never shut to thee."

Mowgli's throat worked, and his voice seemed to be dragged from it as he answered, "I will surely come back.

"And now," he said, as he put by the head of the fawning wolf on the threshold, "I have a little cry against thee, Gray Brother. Why came ye not all four when I called so long ago?"

"So long ago? It was but last night. We were singing in the Jungle the new songs, for this is the Time of New Talk. Rememberest thou?"

"Truly, truly."

"And as soon as the songs were sung," Gray Brother went on earnestly, "I followed thy trail. But, O Little Brother, what hast *thou* done, eating and sleeping with the Man Pack?"

"If ye had come when I called, this had never been," said Mowgli, as he ran with Gray Brother.

"And now what is to be?" said Gray Brother.

Mowgli was going to answer when a girl in a white cloth came down some path that led from the outskirts of the village. Gray Brother dropped out of sight at once, and Mowgli backed noiselessly into a field of high-springing crops. He could almost have touched her with his hand when the warm, green stalks closed before his face and he disappeared like a ghost. The girl screamed, for she thought she had seen a spirit, and then she gave a deep sigh. Mowgli parted the stalks with his hands and watched her till she was out of sight.

"And now I do not know," he said, sighing in his turn. "*Why did ye not come when I called?*"

"We follow thee—we follow thee," Gray Brother mumbled, licking at Mowgli's heel. "We follow thee always, except in the Time of the New Talk."

"And would ye follow me to the Man Pack?" Mowgli whispered.

"Did I not follow thee on the night our old Pack cast thee out? Have I not followed thee tonight?"

"Ay, but again and again, and it may be again, Gray Brother?"

Gray Brother was silent. When he spoke he growled to himself. "The Black One spoke truth."

"And he said?"

"Man goes to Man at the last."

"So also said Akela on the night of Red Dog," Mowgli muttered. "What dost thou say, Gray Brother?"

"They cast thee out once, with bad talk. They cut thy mouth with stones. Thou, and not I, didst make song against them more bitter even than our song against Red Dog."

"I ask thee what *thou* sayest?"

They were talking as they ran. Gray Brother cantered on a while without replying, and then he said—between bound and bound as it were—"Man-cub—Master of the Jungle—lair brother to me—though I forget for a little while in the spring, thy trail is my trail, thy lair is my lair, thy kill is my kill, and thy death fight is my death fight. I speak for the Three. But what wilt thou say to the Jungle?"

"That is well thought. Go before and cry them all to the Council Rock, and I will tell them what is in my stomach. But they may not come—in the Time of New Talk they may forget me."

"Hast *thou*, then, forgotten nothing?" snapped Gray Brother over his shoulder, as he laid himself down to gallop, and Mowgli followed, thinking.

At any other season the news would have called all the Jungle together with bristling necks, but now they were busy hunting and fighting and killing and singing. From one to another Gray Brother ran, crying, "The Master of the Jungle goes back to Man! Come to the Council Rock." And the happy, eager People only answered, "He will return in the summer heats. The Rains will drive him to lair. Run and sing with us, Gray Brother."

"But the Master of the Jungle goes back to Man," Gray Brother would repeat.

"*Eee—Yoawa?* Is the Time of New Talk any less sweet for that?" they would reply. So when Mowgli, heavyhearted, came up through the well-remembered rocks to the place where he had been brought into the Council, he found only the Four, Baloo, who was nearly blind with age, and the heavy, cold-blooded Kaa coiled around Akela's empty seat.

"Thy trail ends here, then, Manling?" said Kaa, as Mowgli threw himself down, his face in his hands. "Cry thy cry. We be of one blood, thou and I—man and snake together."

"Why did I not die under Red Dog?" the boy moaned. "My strength is gone from me. By night and by day I hear a double step upon my trail. When I turn my head it is as though one had hidden himself from me that instant. I go to look behind the trees and he is not there. I call and none cry again; but it is as though one listened and kept back the answer. I run the spring running, but I am not made still. I bathe, but I am not made cool. The kill sickens me, but I have no heart to fight except I kill. The Red Flower is in my body, my bones are water—and—I know not what I know."

"What need of talk?" said Baloo slowly, turning his head to where Mowgli lay. "Akela by the river said it, that Mowgli should drive Mowgli back to the Man Pack. I said it. But who listens now to Baloo? Bagheera—where is Bagheera this night?—he knows also. It is the Law."

"When we met at Cold Lairs, Manling, I knew it," said Kaa,

turning a little in his mighty coils. "Man goes to Man at the last, though the Jungle does not cast him out."

The Four looked at one another and at Mowgli, puzzled but obedient.

"The Jungle does not cast me out, then?" Mowgli stammered.

Gray Brother and the Three growled furiously, beginning, "So long as we live none shall dare—"

But Baloo checked them. "I taught thee the Law. It is for me to speak," he said; "and, though I cannot now see the rocks before me, I see far. Little Frog, take thine own trail; make thy lair with thine own blood and pack and people; but when there is need of foot or tooth or eye, remember, Master of the Jungle, the Jungle is thine at call."

"*Hai-mai*, my brothers," cried Mowgli, throwing up his arms with a sob. "I know not what I know! I would not go; but I am drawn by both feet. How shall I leave these nights?"

"Listen, dearest of all to me," said Baloo. "There is neither word nor will here to hold thee back. Look up! Who may question the Master of the Jungle? I saw thee playing among the white pebbles yonder when thou wast a little frog; and Bagheera saw thee also. Of that Looking-over we two only remain; for Raksha, thy lair mother, is dead with thy lair father; the old Wolf Pack is long since dead; thou knowest whither Shere Khan went, and Akela died among the dholes, where, but for thy wisdom and strength, the second Seeonee Pack would also have died. There remains nothing but old bones. It is no longer the Man-cub that asks leave of his Pack, but the Master of the Jungle that changes his trail. Who shall question Man in his ways?"

"But Bagheera and the Bull that bought me," said Mowgli. "I would not—"

His words were cut short by a roar and a crash in the thicket below, and Bagheera, light, strong, and terrible as always, stood before him.

"*Therefore*," he said, stretching out a dripping right paw, "I did not come. It was a long hunt, but he lies dead in the bushes now—a bull in his second year—the Bull that frees thee, Little Brother.

All debts are paid now. For the rest, my word is Baloo's word." He licked Mowgli's foot. "Remember, Bagheera loved thee," he cried, and bounded away. At the foot of the hill he cried again long and loud, "Good hunting on a new trail, Master of the Jungle! Remember, Bagheera loved thee."

"Thou hast heard," said Baloo. "There is no more. Go now; but first come to me. O wise Little Frog, come to me!"

"It is hard to cast the skin," said Kaa as Mowgli sobbed and sobbed, with his head on the blind bear's side and his arms round his neck.

"The stars are thin," said Gray Brother, snuffing at the dawn wind. "Where shall we lair today? For, from now, we follow new trails."

.   .   .   .   .

And this is the last of the Mowgli stories.

THE WHITE SEAL

h! hush thee, my baby, the night is behind us,
    And black are the waters that sparkled so green.
The moon, o'er the combers, looks downward to find us
    At rest in the hollows that rustle between.
Where billow meets billow, there soft be thy pillow;
    Ah, weary wee flipperling, curl at thy ease!
The storm shall not wake thee, nor shark overtake thee,
    Asleep in the arms of the slow-swinging seas.
                    Seal Lullaby.

ALL THESE THINGS happened several years ago at a place called Novastoshnah, or North-East Point, on the Island of Saint Paul, away and away in the Bering Sea. Nobody comes to Novastoshnah except on business, and the only people who have regular business there are the seals. They come in the summer months by hundreds of thousands out of the cold gray sea; for Novastoshnah Beach has the finest accommodation for seals of any place in all the world.

Sea Catch knew that, and every spring would swim there like a torpedo boat from whatever place he happened to be in, and spend a month fighting with his companions for a good place on the rocks as close to the sea as possible. Sea Catch was fifteen years old, a huge gray fur seal with almost a mane on his shoulders, and long, wicked dog-teeth. When he heaved himself up on his front flippers he stood more than four feet clear of the ground, and his weight was nearly seven hundred pounds. He was scarred all over with the marks of savage fights, but he was always ready for just one fight more. He would put his head on one side, as though he were afraid to look his enemy in the face; then he would shoot it out like lightning, and when the big teeth were firmly fixed on the other seal's neck, the other seal might get away if he could, but Sea Catch would not help him.

Yet Sea Catch never chased a beaten seal, for that was against the Rules of the Beach. He only wanted room by the sea for his nursery; but as there were forty or fifty thousand other seals hunting for the same thing each spring, the whistling, bellowing, roaring, and blowing on the beach were something frightful.

From a little hill called Hutchinson's Hill you could look over three and a half miles of ground covered with fighting seals; and the surf was dotted all over with the heads of seals hurrying to land and begin their share of the fighting; for they were just as stupid and unaccommodating as men. Their wives never came to the island until late in May or early in June, for they did not care to be torn to pieces; and the young seals who had not begun housekeeping went inland about half a mile through the ranks of the fighters and played about on the sand dunes. They were called the holluschickie—the bachelors—and there were perhaps two or three hundred thousand of them at Novastoshnah alone.

Sea Catch had just finished his forty-fifth fight one spring when Matkah, his sleek, gentle-eyed wife, came up out of the sea, and he caught her by the scruff of the neck and dumped her on his reservation, saying gruffly: "Late, as usual. Where *have* you been?"

It was not the fashion for Sea Catch to eat anything during the four months he stayed on the beaches, and so his temper was generally bad. Matkah knew better than to answer back. She looked round and cooed: "How thoughtful of you! You've taken the old place again."

"I should think I had," said Sea Catch. "Look at me!"

He was scratched and bleeding in twenty places; one eye was almost blind, and his sides were torn to ribbons.

"Oh, you men, you men!" Matkah said. "Why can't you be sensible and settle your places quietly? You look as though you had been fighting with the Killer Whale."

"I haven't been doing anything *but* fight since the middle of May. The beach is disgracefully crowded this season."

Sea Catch pretended to go to sleep for a few minutes, but all the time he was keeping a sharp lookout for a fight. Now that all the seals and their wives were on the land, you could hear their clamor miles out to sea above the loudest gales. At the lowest counting there were over a million seals on the beach, fighting, scuffling, bleating, crawling, and playing together—going down to the sea and coming up from it in gangs and regiments, and skirmishing about in brigades through the fog. It is nearly always foggy at Novastoshnah, except when the sun comes out and makes everything look all pearly and rainbow-colored for a little while.

Kotick, Matkah's baby, was born in the middle of that confusion, and he was all head and shoulders, with pale, watery-blue eyes and white fur, as tiny seals must be. She sang to him the low, crooning seal song that all the mother seals sing to their babies:

> "*You mustn't swim till you're six weeks old,*
>   *Or your head will be sunk by your heels;*
>   *And summer gales and Killer Whales*
>   *Are bad for baby seals.*
>
> "*Are bad for baby seals, dear rat,*
>   *As bad as bad can be;*
>   *But splash and grow strong,*
>   *And you can't be wrong,*
>   *Child of the Open Sea!*"

Of course the little fellow did not understand the words at first. He paddled and scrambled about by his mother's side, and learned to scuffle out of the way when his father was fighting with another seal. Matkah used to go to sea to get things to eat, and the baby was fed only once in two days; but then he ate all he could, and throve upon it.

The first thing he did was to crawl inland, and there he met tens of thousands of babies of his own age, and they played together like puppies, went to sleep on the clean sand, and played again.

When Matkah came back from her deep-sea fishing she would go straight to their playground and call as a sheep calls for a lamb, and wait until she heard Kotick bleat. Then she would take a straight line in his direction, striking out with her fore flippers and knocking the youngsters head over heels right and left.

Little seals can no more swim than little children, but they are unhappy till they learn. The first time that Kotick went down to the sea a wave carried him out beyond his depth, and his big head sank and his little hind flippers flew up exactly as his mother had told him, and if the next wave had not thrown him back again he would have drowned. After that he learned to lie in a beach pool and let the wash of the waves just cover him and lift him up while he paddled, but he always kept his eye open for big waves that might hurt. He was two weeks learning to use his flippers; and all that while he floundered in and out of the water, until at last he found that he truly belonged to it.

Then you can imagine the times that he had with his companions, ducking under the rollers; or coming in on top of a comber and landing with a swash and a splutter as the big wave went whirling far up the beach; or playing "I'm the King of the Castle" on slippery, weedy rocks that just stuck out of the wash. Now and then he would see a thin fin drifting along close to shore, and he knew that that was the Killer Whale who eats young seals when he can get them; and Kotick would head for the beach like an arrow, and the fin would jig off slowly, as if it were looking for nothing at all. In time the other young seals began to take on the color of their parents. But not Kotick. There was something about his coat that made his mother look at him very closely.

"Sea Catch," she said at last, "our baby's going to be white."

"Empty clamshells and dry seaweed!" snorted Sea Catch. "There never has been such a thing in the world as a white seal."

"I can't help that," said Matkah; "there's going to be now."

Late in October the seals began to leave Saint Paul's for the deep sea, and there was no more fighting over the nurseries, and the holluschickie played anywhere they liked. "Next year," said Matkah to Kotick, "you will be a holluschick; but this year you must learn how to catch fish."

They set out together across the Pacific, and Matkah showed Kotick how to sleep on his back with his flippers tucked down by his side and his little nose just out of the water. No cradle is so comfortable as the long, rocking swell of the Pacific. When Kotick felt his skin tingle all over, Matkah told him he was learning the "feel of the water," and that tingly, prickly feelings meant bad weather coming, and he must swim hard and get away.

"In a little time," she said, "you'll know where to swim to, but just now we'll follow Sea Pig, the Porpoise, for he is very wise." A school of porpoises were ducking and tearing through the water, and little Kotick followed them as fast as he could. "How do you know where to go?" he panted. The leader of the school rolled his white eyes, and ducked under. "My tail tingles, youngster," he said. "That means there's a gale behind me. Come along! When you're south of the Sticky Water [he meant the Equator], and your tail tingles, that means there's a gale in front of you and you must head north. Come along!"

This was one of the very many things that Kotick learned. Matkah taught him to follow the cod and the halibut along the undersea banks, and wrench the rockling out of his hole among the weeds; how to dance on the top of the waves when the lightning was racing all over the sky; how to jump three or four feet clear of the water, like a dolphin, flippers close to the side and tail curved; to leave the flying fish alone because they are all bony; and never to stop and look at a boat or a ship. At the end of six months, what Kotick did not know about deep-sea fishing was not worth the knowing, and all that time he never set flipper on dry ground.

One day, however, as he was lying half asleep in the warm water somewhere off the Islands of Juan Fernández, he felt faint and lazy all over, just as human people do when the spring is in their legs, and he remembered the good firm beaches of Novastoshnah seven thousand miles away, the games his companions played, the smell of the seaweed, the seal roar, and the fighting. That very minute he turned north, swimming steadily, and as he went on he met scores of his mates, all bound for the same place, and they said: "Greeting, Kotick! This year we are all holluschickie, and we can dance the Fire Dance and play on the new grass. But where did you get that coat?"

Kotick's fur was still almost pure white, and though he felt very proud of it, he only said: "Swim quickly! My bones are aching for the land." And so they all came to the beaches where they had been born, and heard their fathers fighting in the rolling mist.

That night Kotick danced the Fire Dance with the yearling seals. The sea is full of fire on summer nights all the way down from Novastoshnah to Lukannon, and each seal leaves a wake like burning oil behind him, and a flaming flash when he jumps, and the waves break in great phosphorescent streaks and swirls. Then they went inland to the holluschickie grounds, and rolled up and down in the new wild wheat, and told stories of what they had done while they had been at sea.

The three- and four-year-old holluschickie romped down from Hutchinson's Hill, crying: "Out of the way, youngsters! The sea is deep, and you don't know all that's in it yet. Hi, you yearling, where did you get that white coat?"

"I didn't get it," said Kotick; "it grew." And just as he was going to roll the speaker over, a couple of black-haired men with flat red faces came from behind a sand dune, and Kotick, who had never seen a man before, coughed and lowered his head. The holluschickie just bundled off a few yards and sat staring stupidly. The men were no less than Kerick Booterin, the chief of the seal hunters on the island, and Patalamon, his son. They came from the little village not half a mile from the seal nurseries, and they were deciding what seals they would drive up to the killing pens to be turned into sealskin jackets later on.

"Ho!" said Patalamon. "Look! There's a white seal!"

Kerick Booterin turned pale under his oil and smoke. Then he began to mutter a prayer. "Don't touch him, Patalamon. There has never been a white seal since—since I was born. Perhaps it is old Zaharrof's ghost. He was lost last year in the big gale."

"I'm not going near him," said Patalamon. "He's unlucky. Do you really think he is old Zaharrof come back?"

"Don't look at him," said Kerick. "Head off that drove of four-year-olds. The men ought to skin two hundred today, but it's the beginning of the season, and they are new to the work. A hundred will do. Quick!"

Patalamon rattled a pair of seal's shoulder bones in front of a herd of holluschickie, and they stopped dead, puffing and blowing. Then he stepped near, and the seals began to move, and Kerick headed them inland, and they never tried to get back to their companions. Hundreds and hundreds of thousands of seals watched them being driven, but they went on playing just the same. Kotick was the only one who asked questions, and none of his companions could tell him anything, except that the men always drove seals in that way for six weeks or two months of every year.

"I am going to follow," he said, and his eyes nearly popped out of his head as he shuffled along in the wake of the herd.

"The white seal is coming after us," cried Patalamon. "That's the first time a seal has ever come to the killing grounds alone."

"Hsh! Don't look behind you," said Kerick. "It *is* Zaharrof's ghost! I must speak to the priest about this."

The distance to the killing grounds was only half a mile, but it took an hour to cover, because if the seals went too fast Kerick knew that they would get heated and then their fur would come off in patches when they were skinned. So they went on very slowly till they came to the Salt House just beyond the sight of the seals on the beach. Kotick followed, panting and wondering. He thought that he was at the world's end, but the roar of the seal nurseries behind him sounded as loud as the roar of a train in a tunnel. Kerick sat down on the moss and let the drove cool off for thirty minutes. Then ten or twelve men, each with an iron-bound club three or four feet long, came up, and Kerick pointed out one or two of the drove that were bitten by their companions or were too hot, and the men kicked those aside, and then Kerick said, "Let go!" and then the men clubbed the seals on the head as fast as they could.

Ten minutes later little Kotick did not recognize his friends anymore, for their skins were ripped off from the nose to the hind flippers—whipped off and thrown down on the ground in a pile.

That was enough for Kotick. He turned and galloped (a seal can gallop very swiftly for a short time) back to the sea, his little new mustache bristling with horror. At Sea-Lion's Neck, where the great sea lions sit on the edge of the surf, he flung himself flipper over head into the cool water, and rocked there, gasping miserably.

"What's here?" said a sea lion gruffly; for as a rule the sea lions keep themselves to themselves.

"I'm lonesome, very lonesome!" said Kotick. "They're killing *all* the holluschickie on *all* the beaches!"

The sea lion turned his head inshore. "Nonsense!" he said; "your friends are making as much noise as ever. You must have seen old Kerick polishing off a drove."

"It's horrible," said Kotick, backing water as a wave went over him, and steadying himself with a screw-stroke of his flippers that brought him up all standing within three inches of a jagged rock.

"Well done for a yearling!" said the sea lion, who could appreciate good swimming. "I suppose it *is* rather awful from your way of looking at it; but if you seals will come here year after year, of course the men get to know of it, and unless you can find an island where no men ever come, you will always be driven."

"Isn't there any such island?" began Kotick.

"I've followed the halibut for twenty years, and I can't say I've found it yet. But look here—suppose you go to Walrus Islet and talk to Sea Vitch. He may know something. Don't flounce off like that. It's a six-mile swim, and if I were you I should haul out and take a nap first, little one."

Kotick thought that that was good advice, so he slept for half an hour. Then he headed straight for Walrus Islet, a little rocky island almost due northeast from Novastoshnah, where the walrus herded by themselves. He landed close to old Sea Vitch—the big, ugly, fat-necked, long-tusked walrus of the North Pacific—who has no manners except when he is asleep, as he was then, with his hind flippers half in and half out of the surf. "Wake up!" barked Kotick, for the gulls were making a great noise.

"Hmph! What's that?" said Sea Vitch, and he struck the next

walrus a blow with his tusks and woke him up, and the next struck the next, and so on till they were all awake and staring in every direction but the right one.

"Hi! It's me," said Kotick, bobbing in the surf and looking like a little white slug.

"Well! May I be—skinned!" said Sea Vitch, and they all looked at Kotick as you can fancy a club full of drowsy old gentlemen would look at a little boy. Kotick did not care to hear any more about skinning just then; so he called out: "Isn't there any place for seals to go where men don't ever come?"

"Go and find out," said Sea Vitch, shutting his eyes. "Run away. We're busy here."

Kotick made his dolphin-jump in the air and shouted as loud as he could: "Clam eater! Clam eater!" He knew that Sea Vitch never caught a fish in his life, but always rooted for clams and seaweeds, though he pretended to be a very terrible person. The Burgomaster Gulls and the Kittiwakes and the Puffins, who are always looking for a chance to be rude, took up the cry, and for nearly five minutes you could not have heard a gun fired on Walrus Islet.

"*Now* will you tell?" said Kotick at last, all out of breath.

"Go and ask Sea Cow," said Sea Vitch. "If he is living still, he'll be able to tell you."

"How shall I know Sea Cow when I meet him?" said Kotick.

"He's the only thing in the sea uglier than Sea Vitch," screamed a Burgomaster Gull. "Uglier, and with worse manners!"

Kotick sheered off and swam back to Novastoshnah, leaving the gulls to scream. There he found that no one sympathized with him in his little attempts to discover a quiet place for the seals. They told him that men had always driven the holluschickie, and that if he did not like to see ugly things he should not have gone to the killing grounds. But none of the other seals had seen the killing, and that made the difference between him and his friends. Besides, Kotick was a white seal.

"What you must do," said old Sea Catch, after he had heard his son's adventures, "is to grow up and be a big seal like your father, and then they will leave you alone. In another five years you ought to be able to fight for yourself." Even gentle Matkah, his mother,

97

said: "You will never be able to stop the killing. Go and play in the sea, Kotick." And Kotick went off and danced the Fire Dance with a very heavy little heart.

That autumn he set off from the beach alone because of a notion in his bullethead. He was going to find Sea Cow, and he was going to find a quiet island with good firm beaches for seals to live on. So he explored by himself from the North to the South Pacific, swimming as much as three hundred miles in a day and a night. He met with more adventures than can be told, and narrowly escaped being caught by the Basking Shark, and the Spotted Shark, and the Hammerhead, and he met all the untrustworthy ruffians that loaf up and down the seas, and the heavy polite fish, and the scarlet-spotted scallops that are moored in one place for hundreds of years, and grow very proud of it; but he never met Sea Cow, and he never found an island that he could fancy.

He picked up with an old stumpy-tailed albatross, who told him that Kerguelen Island was the very place for peace and quiet, and when Kotick went down there he was all but smashed to pieces against some wicked black cliffs in a heavy sleet storm. Yet as he pulled out against the gale he could see that there had once been a seal nursery there. And so it was in all the other islands he visited.

Kotick spent five seasons exploring, with a four months' rest each year at Novastoshnah. He went to the Galápagos, a horrid dry place on the Equator, where he was nearly baked to death; he went to the Georgia Islands, the South Orkneys, little Nightingale Island, the Crossets, and even to a little speck of an island south of the Cape of Good Hope. But everywhere the People of the Sea told him the same things. Seals had come to those islands once upon a time, but men had killed them all off. Even when he swam thousands of miles out of the Pacific, and got to a place called Cape Corrientes, he found a few hundred mangy seals on a rock, and they told him that men came there too.

That nearly broke his heart, and he headed round the Horn back to his own beaches; and on his way north he hauled out on an island where he found an old, old seal who was dying, and Kotick caught fish for him and told him all his sorrows. "Now," said Kotick, "I am going back to Novastoshnah, and if I am driven to the killing pens I shall not care."

The old seal said: "Try once more. I am the last of the Lost Rookery of Más Afuera, and in the days when men killed us by the hundred thousand there was a story on the beaches that some day a white seal would come out of the north and lead the seal people to a quiet place. I am old and I shall never live to see that day, but others will. Try once more."

And Kotick curled up his mustache (it was a beauty), and said, "I am the only white seal in the world, and I am the only seal who ever thought of looking for new islands."

That cheered him immensely; and when he came back to Novastoshnah that summer, Matkah, his mother, begged him to marry and settle down, for he was now full grown, with a curly white mane on his shoulders, as heavy, as big, and as fierce as his father. "Give me another season," he said. "Remember, Mother, it is always the seventh wave that goes farthest up the beach."

Curiously enough, there was another seal who thought that she would put off marrying till the next year, and Kotick danced the Fire Dance with her all down Lukannon Beach the night before he set off on his last exploration.

This time he went westward, because he had fallen on the trail of a great shoal of halibut, and he needed at least one hundred pounds of fish a day to keep him in good condition. He chased them till he was tired, and then he curled himself up and went to sleep on the hollows of the ground swell that sets in to Copper Island. He knew the coast well, so about midnight, when he felt himself gently bumped on a weed bed, he said, "Hm, tide's running strong," and turning over under water opened his eyes slowly and stretched. Then he jumped like a cat, for he saw huge things nosing about in the shoal water and browsing on the heavy fringes of the weeds.

"By the Great Combers of Magellan!" he said beneath his mustache. "Who in the Deep Sea are these people?"

They were like no people that Kotick had ever seen before. They were between twenty and thirty feet long, and they had no hind flippers, but a shovel-like tail that looked as if it had been whittled out of wet leather. They balanced on the ends of their tails in deep water when they weren't grazing, bowing solemnly to one another and waving their front flippers as a fat man waves his arm.

"Ahem!" said Kotick. "Good sport, gentlemen?" The big things answered by bowing and waving their flippers. When they began feeding again Kotick saw that their upper lip was split into two pieces that they could twitch apart about a foot and bring together again with a whole bushel of seaweed between the splits. They tucked the stuff into their mouths and chumped solemnly.

"Messy style of feeding, that," said Kotick. They bowed again, and Kotick began to lose his temper. "Very good," he said. "I see you bow gracefully, but I should like to know your names." The split lips moved and twitched, and the glassy green eyes stared; but they did not speak.

"Well!" said Kotick. "You're the only people I've ever met uglier than Sea Vitch—and with worse manners." Then he remembered in a flash what the Burgomaster Gull had screamed to him when he was a little yearling at Walrus Islet, and he tumbled backward in the water, for he knew that he had found Sea Cow at last.

The sea cows went on schlooping and chumping in the weed, and Kotick asked them questions in every language that he had picked up in his travels. But the Sea Cow did not answer, because Sea Cow cannot talk.

By daylight Kotick's mane was standing on end and his temper was gone. Then the Sea Cow began to travel northward very slowly, stopping to hold absurd bowing councils from time to time, and Kotick followed them, saying to himself: "People who are such idiots as these are would have been killed long ago if they hadn't found some safe island; and what is good enough for the Sea Cow is good enough for the Sea Catch. All the same, I wish they'd hurry."

It was weary work for Kotick. The herd never went more than forty or fifty miles a day, and stopped to feed at night, and kept close to the shore all the time; while Kotick swam round them, and over them, and under them, but he could not hurry them on one half-mile. They held a bowing council every few hours, and Kotick nearly bit off his mustache with impatience till he saw that they were following up a warm current of water, and then he respected them more.

One night they sank through the shiny water—sank like stones—and, for the first time since he had known them, began to swim quickly. Kotick followed, and the pace astonished him. They headed for a cliff that ran down into deep water, and plunged into a dark hole at the foot of it, twenty fathoms under the sea. It was a long, long swim, and Kotick badly wanted fresh air before he was out of the dark tunnel that they led him through.

"My wig!" he said, when he rose, gasping and puffing, into open water at the farther end. "It was a long dive, but it was worth it."

The sea cows had separated, and were browsing lazily along the edges of the finest beaches that Kotick had ever seen. There were long stretches of smooth-worn rock running for miles, exactly fitted to make seal nurseries, and there were playgrounds of hard sand sloping inland behind them, and there were rollers for seals to dance in, and sand dunes to climb up and down; and, best of all, Kotick knew by the feel of the water, which never deceives a true Sea Catch, that no men had ever come there.

The first thing he did was to assure himself that the fishing was good, and then he swam along the beaches and counted up the delightful low sandy islands half hidden in the beautiful rolling fog. Away to the northward out to sea ran a line of shoals and rocks that would never let a ship come within six miles of the beach; and between the islands and the mainland was a stretch of deep water that ran up to the perpendicular cliffs.

"It's Novastoshnah over again, but ten times better," said Kotick. "Men can't come down the cliffs, even if there were any men; and the shoals to seaward would knock a ship to splinters. If any place in the sea is safe, this is it."

Though he was in a hurry to go back to Novastoshnah, he thoroughly explored the new country, so that he would be able to answer all questions. Then he dived and made sure of the mouth of the tunnel, and raced through to the southward. No one but a sea cow or a seal would have dreamed of there being such a place, and when he looked back at the cliffs even Kotick could hardly believe that he had been under them.

He was six days going home, though he was not swimming slowly; and when he hauled out just above Sea-Lion's Neck the first person he met was the seal who had been waiting for him, and she saw by the look in his eyes that he had found his island at last.

But the holluschickie and his father, and all the other seals, laughed at him when he told them what he had discovered, and a young seal about his own age said: "That is all very well, Kotick, but you can't come and order us off like this. Remember we've been fighting for our nurseries, and that's a thing you never did. You preferred prowling about in the sea."

The other seals laughed at this, and the young seal began twisting his head from side to side. He had just married that year, and was making a great fuss about it.

"I've no nursery to fight for," said Kotick. "I want only to show you all a place where you will be safe. What's the use of fighting?"

"Oh, if you're trying to back out, of course I've no more to say," said the young seal, with an ugly chuckle.

"Will you come with me if I win?" said Kotick; and a green light came into his eyes, for he was very angry at having to fight at all.

"Very good," said the young seal. "*If* you win, I'll come."

He had no time to change his mind, for Kotick's head darted out and his teeth sank in the blubber of the young seal's neck. Then he threw himself back on his haunches and hauled his enemy down the beach, shook him, and knocked him over. Then Kotick roared to the seals: "I've done my best for you these five seasons past. I've found you the island where you'll be safe, but unless your heads are dragged off your silly necks you won't believe. I'm going to teach you now. Look out for yourselves!"

Kotick flung himself at the biggest seal he could find, caught him by the throat, choked him and bumped him and banged him till he grunted for mercy, and then threw him aside and attacked the next. You see, Kotick had never fasted for four months as the big seals did every year, and his deep-sea swimming trips kept him in perfect condition. His curly white mane stood up with rage, and his eyes flamed, and he was splendid to look at.

Old Sea Catch, his father, saw him tearing past, hauling the grizzled old seals about as though they had been halibut, and up-setting the young bachelors in all directions; and Sea Catch gave one roar and shouted: "He may be a fool, but he is the best fighter on the beaches. Don't tackle your father, my son! He's with you!"

Kotick roared in answer, and old Sea Catch waddled in, blowing like a locomotive, while Matkah and the seal that was going to marry Kotick cowered down and admired their menfolk. It was a gorgeous fight, for the two fought as long as there was a seal that dared lift up his head, and then they paraded grandly up and down the beach side by side, bellowing.

At night, just as the Northern Lights were winking and flashing through the fog, Kotick climbed a bare rock and looked down on the torn and bleeding seals. "Now," he said, "I've taught you your lesson."

"My wig!" said old Sea Catch, boosting himself up stiffly, for he was fearfully mauled. "The Killer Whale himself could not have cut them up worse. Son, I'm proud of you, and what's more, I'll come with you to your island."

"Here you, fat pigs of the sea! Who comes with me to the Sea Cow's tunnel?" roared Kotick.

There was a murmur like the ripple of the tide all up and down the beaches. "We will come," said thousands of tired voices. "We will follow Kotick, the White Seal."

Then Kotick dropped his head between his shoulders and shut his eyes proudly. He was not a white seal anymore, but red from head to tail. All the same, he would have scorned to look at or touch one of his wounds.

A week later he and his army (nearly ten thousand holluschickie and old seals) went away north to the Sea Cow's tunnel, and the seals that stayed at Novastoshnah called them idiots. But next spring, when they all met off the fishing banks of the Pacific, Kotick's seals told such tales of the new beaches beyond the Sea Cow's tunnel that more and more seals left Novastoshnah.

Of course it was not all done at once, for the seals need a long time to turn things over in their minds, but year by year more seals went away from Novastoshnah to the quiet, sheltered beaches where Kotick sits all the summer through, getting bigger and fatter and stronger each year, while the holluschickie play round him, in that sea where no man comes.

THIS IS THE STORY of the great war that Rikki-tikki-tavi fought single-handed, through the bathrooms of the big bungalow in Segowlee cantonment. Darzee, the tailorbird, and Chuchundra, the muskrat, helped him, but Rikki-tikki did the real fighting.

He was a mongoose, rather like a little cat in his fur and his tail, but quite like a weasel in his head and his habits. His eyes and the end of his restless nose were pink; he could scratch himself anywhere he pleased, with any leg that he chose to use; he could fluff up his tail till it looked like a bottle brush, and his war cry, as he scuttled through the long grass, was "*Rikk-tikk-tikki-tikki-tchk!*"

One day, a high summer flood washed him out of the burrow where he lived with his father and mother, and carried him, kicking and clucking, down a roadside ditch. He found a little wisp of grass floating there, and clung to it till he lost his senses. When he revived, he was lying in the hot sun on the middle of a garden path, very draggled indeed, and a small boy was saying: "Here's a dead mongoose. Let's have a funeral."

"No," said his mother; "let's take him in and dry him. Perhaps he isn't really dead."

They took him into the house, and a big man picked him up between his finger and thumb and said he was not dead but half choked; so they wrapped him in cotton wool, and warmed him, and he opened his eyes and sneezed.

"Now," said the big man (he was an Englishman who had just

moved into the bungalow); "don't frighten him, and we'll see what he'll do."

It is the hardest thing in the world to frighten a mongoose, because he is filled with curiosity. Rikki-tikki looked at the cotton wool, decided it was not good to eat, ran all round the table, sat up and put his fur in order, and jumped on the small boy's shoulder.

"That's his way of making friends, Teddy," said his father.

"Ouch! He's tickling under my chin," said Teddy.

Rikki-tikki looked down between the boy's collar and neck, snuffed at his ear, and climbed down to the floor, where he sat rubbing his nose.

"Good gracious," said Teddy's mother, "and that's a wild creature! I suppose he's so tame because we've been kind to him."

"Mongooses are like that," said her husband. "If we don't pick him up by the tail, or try to put him in a cage, he'll run in and out of the house all day long. Let's give him something to eat."

They gave him a little piece of raw meat. Rikki-tikki liked it immensely, and when it was finished he went out into the veranda and sat in the sunshine and fluffed up his fur to make it dry to the roots. Then he felt better.

He spent all day roaming over the house. He nearly drowned himself in the bathtubs, put his nose into the ink on a writing table, and burned it on the end of the big man's cigar, for he climbed up in the man's lap to see how writing was done. When Teddy went to bed Rikki-tikki climbed up too; but he was a restless companion, because he had to get up and find out what made every noise all through the night. Teddy's parents came in to look at their boy, and Rikki-tikki was awake on the pillow. "He may bite the child," said the mother. "He'll do no such thing," said the father. "Teddy's safer with that little beast than if he had a bloodhound to watch him. If a snake came into the nursery now—"

But Teddy's mother wouldn't think of anything so awful.

Early in the morning Rikki-tikki came to breakfast in the veranda riding on Teddy's shoulder, and they gave him banana and some boiled egg. Then he went out into the garden to see what was to be seen. It was a large garden, only half cultivated, with bushes as big as summerhouses of Marshal Niel roses, lime and orange trees, clumps of bamboos, and thickets of high grass. Rikki-tikki licked his lips. "This is a splendid hunting ground," he said, and his tail grew bottle-brushy at the thought of it, and he scuttled up and down the garden, snuffing here and there till he heard very sorrowful voices in a thornbush.

It was Darzee, the tailorbird, and his wife. They had made a beautiful nest by pulling two big leaves together and stitching them up the edges with fibers, and had filled the hollow with cotton and downy fluff. The nest swayed to and fro, as they sat on the rim and cried.

"What is the matter?" asked Rikki-tikki.

"We are very miserable," said Darzee. "One of our babies fell out of the nest yesterday, and Nag ate him."

"H'm!" said Rikki-tikki, "that is very sad—but I am a stranger here. Who is Nag?"

Darzee and his wife only cowered down in the nest without answering, for from the thick grass at the foot of the bush there came a low hiss—a horrid cold sound that made Rikki-tikki jump back two clear feet. Then inch by inch out of the grass rose up the spread hood of Nag, the big black cobra, and he was five feet long from tongue to tail. When he had lifted one third of himself clear of the ground, he stayed balancing to and fro exactly as a dandelion tuft balances in the wind, and he looked at Rikki-tikki with the wicked snake's eyes that never change expression.

"Who is Nag?" said he. "*I* am Nag. The great god Brahm put his mark upon all our people when the first cobra spread his hood to keep the sun off Brahm as he slept. Look, and be afraid!"

He spread out his hood more than ever, and Rikki-tikki saw the spectacle-mark on the back of it that looks exactly like the eye part of a hook-and-eye fastening. He was afraid for the minute; but it is impossible for a mongoose to stay frightened for any length of time, and though Rikki-tikki had never met a live cobra before, his mother had fed him on dead ones, and he knew that all a grown mongoose's business in life was to fight and eat snakes.

"Well," said Rikki-tikki, and his tail began to fluff up again, "marks or no marks, do you think it is right for you to eat fledglings out of a nest?"

Nag was thinking to himself, and watching the least little movement in the grass behind Rikki-tikki. He knew that mongooses in the garden meant death sooner or later for him and his family, but he wanted to get Rikki-tikki off his guard. So he dropped his head a little, and put it on one side. "Let us talk," he said. "You eat eggs. Why should not I eat birds?"

"Behind you! Look behind you!" sang Darzee.

Rikki-tikki knew better than to waste time in staring. He jumped up in the air as high as he could go, and just under him whizzed by the head of Nagaina, Nag's wicked wife. She had crept up behind him as he was talking, to make an end of him; and he heard her savage hiss as the stroke missed. He came down almost across her back, and if he had been an old mongoose he would have known that then was the time to break her back with one bite; but he was afraid of the terrible lashing return-stroke of the cobra. He bit, indeed, but did not bite long enough, and he jumped clear of the whisking tail, leaving Nagaina torn and angry.

"Wicked, wicked Darzee!" said Nag, lashing up as high as he could reach toward the nest in the thornbush; but Darzee had built it out of reach of snakes, and it only swayed to and fro.

Rikki-tikki felt his eyes growing red and hot (when a mongoose's eyes grow red, he is angry), and he sat back on his tail and hind legs like a little kangaroo, and looked all round him, and chattered with rage. But Nag and Nagaina had disappeared into the grass. Rikki-tikki did not care to follow them, for he did not feel sure that he could manage two snakes at once. So he trotted off to the gravel path near the house, and sat down to think.

The old books of natural history say that when the mongoose fights the snake and happens to get bitten, he runs off and eats some herb that cures him. That is not true. The victory is only a matter of quickness—snake's blow against mongoose's jump—and as no eye can follow the motion of a snake's head when it strikes, that makes things much more wonderful than any magic herb. Rikki-tikki knew he was a young mongoose, and it made him all the more pleased to think that he had managed to escape a blow from behind. It gave him confidence in himself, and when Teddy came running down the path, Rikki-tikki was ready to be petted.

But just as Teddy was stooping, something flinched a little in the dust, and a tiny voice said: "Be careful. I am death!" It was Karait, the dusty brown snakeling that lies for choice on the dusty earth; and his bite is as dangerous as the cobra's. But he is so small that nobody thinks of him, and so he does the more harm to people.

Rikki-tikki's eyes grew red again, and he danced up to Karait with the peculiar rocking, swaying motion that he had inherited from his family. It looks very funny, but it is so perfectly balanced a gait that you can fly off from it at any angle you please; and in dealing with snakes this is an advantage. If Rikki-tikki had only known, he was doing a much more dangerous thing than fighting Nag, for Karait is so small, and can turn so quickly, that unless Rikki bit him close to the back of the head, he would get the return-stroke in his eye or lip. But Rikki did not know: he rocked back and forth, looking for a good place to hold. Karait struck out. Rikki jumped sideways and tried to run in, but the wicked little head lashed within a fraction of his shoulder, and he had to jump over the body, and the head followed his heels close.

Teddy shouted to the house: "Oh, look here! Our mongoose is killing a snake"; and Rikki-tikki heard a scream from Teddy's mother. His father ran out with a stick, but by the time he came up, Karait had lunged out once too far, and Rikki-tikki had sprung, jumped on the snake's back, dropped his head far between his forelegs, bitten as high up the back as he could get hold, and rolled away. That bite paralyzed Karait, and Rikki-tikki was just going to eat him up from the tail, after the dinner custom of his family, when he remembered that a full meal makes a slow mongoose, and if he wanted all his strength and quickness ready, he must keep himself thin. He went away for a dust bath under the castor-oil bushes, and then Teddy's mother picked him up and hugged him, crying that he had saved Teddy from death, and Teddy looked on with big scared eyes. Rikki-tikki was rather amused at all the fuss. He was thoroughly enjoying himself.

That night, at dinner, walking to and fro among the wineglasses on the table, he could have stuffed himself three times over with nice things; but he remembered Nag and Nagaina, and though it was very pleasant to be petted by Teddy's mother, and to sit on Teddy's shoulder, his eyes would get red from time to time, and he would go off into his long war cry of "*Rikk-tikk-tikki-tikki-tchk!*"

Teddy carried him off to bed, and insisted on Rikki-tikki sleeping under his chin. Rikki-tikki was too well-bred to bite or scratch, but as soon as Teddy was asleep he went off for his nightly walk round the house, and in the dark he ran up against Chuchundra, the muskrat, creeping round by the wall. Chuchundra is a broken-hearted little beast. He whimpers all night, trying to make up his mind to run into the middle of the room, but he never gets there.

"Don't kill me," said Chuchundra, almost weeping. "Rikki-tikki, don't kill me."

"Do you think a snake-killer kills muskrats?" said Rikki-tikki scornfully.

"Those who kill snakes get killed by snakes," said Chuchundra, more sorrowfully than ever. "And how am I to be sure that Nag won't mistake me for you some dark night?"

"There's not the least danger," said Rikki-tikki; "but Nag is in the garden, and I know you don't go there."

"My cousin Chua, the rat in the garden, told me—" said Chuchundra, and then he stopped.

"Told you what?"

"H'sh! Nag is everywhere. You should have talked to Chua."

"I didn't—so you must tell me. Quick, or I'll bite you!"

Chuchundra sat down and cried till the tears rolled off his whiskers. "I am a very poor man," he sobbed. "I never had spirit enough to run out into the middle of the room. H'sh! I mustn't tell you anything. Can't you *hear*, Rikki-tikki?"

Rikki-tikki listened. The house was as still as still, but Rikki-tikki thought he could just catch the faintest *scratch-scratch* in the world—a noise as faint as that of a wasp walking on a window-pane—the dry scratch of a snake's scales on brickwork.

"That's Nag or Nagaina," he said to himself; "and he is crawling into the bathroom sluice. You're right, Chuchundra; I should have talked to Chua."

He stole off to Teddy's bathroom, but there was nothing there, and then to Teddy's mother's bathroom. At the bottom of the smooth plaster wall there was a brick pulled out to make a sluice for the bath water, and as Rikki-tikki stole in by the masonry curb where the bath is put, he heard Nag and Nagaina whispering together outside in the moonlight.

"Go in quietly," said Nagaina to her husband, "and remember that the big man is the first one to bite. Then come out and tell me, and we will hunt for Rikki-tikki together."

"But are you sure that there is anything to be gained by killing the people?" said Nag.

"Everything. When there were no people in the bungalow, did we have any mongoose in the garden? So long as the bungalow is empty, we are king and queen of the garden; and remember that as soon as our eggs in the melon bed hatch, our children will need room and quiet."

"I had not thought of that," said Nag. "I will go, but there is no need that we should hunt for Rikki-tikki afterward. I will kill the big man and his wife, and the child if I can, and come away quietly. Then the bungalow will be empty, and Rikki-tikki will go."

Rikki-tikki tingled all over with rage and hatred at this, and then Nag's head came through the sluice, and his five feet of cold body followed it. Angry as he was, Rikki-tikki was very frightened as he saw the size of the big cobra. Nag coiled himself up, raised his head, and looked into the bathroom in the dark, and Rikki could see his eyes glitter.

"Now, if I kill him here, Nagaina will know; and if I fight him on the open floor, the odds are in his favor. What am I to do?" said Rikki-tikki-tavi.

Nag waved to and fro, and then Rikki-tikki heard him drinking from the biggest water jar that was used to fill the bath. "That is good," said the snake. "Now, I shall wait here till the big man comes to bathe in the morning. Nagaina—do you hear me?—I shall wait here in the cool till daytime."

There was no answer from outside, so Rikki-tikki knew Nagaina had gone away. Nag coiled himself down, coil by coil, round the bulge at the bottom of the water jar, and Rikki-tikki stayed still as death. After an hour he began to move, muscle by muscle, toward the jar. Nag was asleep, and Rikki-tikki looked at his big back, wondering which would be the best place for a good hold. "If I don't break his back at the first jump," said Rikki, "he can still fight; and if he fights—O Rikki!" He looked at the thickness of the neck below the hood, but that was too much for him; and a bite near the tail would only make Nag savage.

"It must be the head above the hood," he said at last; "and when I am once there, I must not let go."

Then he jumped. The head was lying a little clear of the water jar, under the curve of it; and, as his teeth met, Rikki braced his back against the bulge of the red earthenware to hold down the head. This gave him just one second's purchase, and he made the most of it. Then he was battered to and fro as a rat is shaken by a dog—to and fro on the floor, up and down, and round in great circles; but his eyes were red, and he held on as the body cartwhipped over the floor, upsetting the dipper and the soap dish, and banged against the tin side of the bath. As he held he closed his jaws tighter and tighter, for he was sure he would be banged to death, and, for the honor of his family, he preferred to be found with his teeth locked. He was dizzy, aching, and felt shaken to pieces when something went off like a thunderclap just behind him; a hot wind knocked him senseless and red fire singed his fur. The big man had been wakened by the noise, and had fired both barrels of a shotgun into Nag just behind the hood.

Rikki-tikki held on with his eyes shut, for now he was quite sure he was dead; but the head did not move, and the big man picked him up and said: "It's the mongoose again, Alice; the little chap has saved *our* lives now." Then Teddy's mother came in with a very white face, and Rikki-tikki dragged himself to Teddy's bedroom and shook himself tenderly to find out whether he really was broken into forty pieces, as he fancied.

When morning came he was very stiff, but well pleased with his doings. "Now I have Nagaina to settle with, and she will be worse than five Nags, and there's no knowing when the eggs she spoke of will hatch. Goodness! I must go and see Darzee," he said.

Rikki-tikki ran to the thornbush where Darzee was singing a song of triumph. The news of Nag's death was all over the garden, for the sweeper had thrown the body on the rubbish heap.

"Oh, you stupid tuft of feathers!" said Rikki-tikki angrily. "Is this the time to sing?"

"Nag is dead!" sang Darzee. "The valiant Rikki-tikki caught him by the head and held fast. The big man brought the bang-stick and Nag fell in two pieces! He will never eat my babies again."

"All that's true enough; but where's Nagaina?" said Rikki-tikki.

"Nagaina came to the bathroom sluice and called for Nag," Darzee went on; "and Nag came out on the end of the sweeper's stick. Let us sing about the great, the red-eyed Rikki-tikki!" and Darzee filled his throat and sang.

"If I could get up to your nest, I'd roll all your babies out!" said Rikki-tikki. "You don't know when to do the right thing at the right time. Stop singing a minute, Darzee."

"For the great, the beautiful Rikki-tikki's sake I will stop," said Darzee. "What is it, O Killer of the terrible Nag?"

"Where is Nagaina, for the second time?"

"On the rubbish heap by the stables, mourning for Nag. Great is Rikki-tikki with the white teeth."

"Bother my white teeth! Have you ever heard where she keeps her eggs?"

"In the melon bed, where the sun strikes nearly all day. She hid them three weeks ago."

"And you never thought it worthwhile to tell me?"

"Rikki-tikki, you are not going to eat her eggs?"

"Not eat exactly; no. Darzee, fly off to the stables and pretend your wing is broken, and let Nagaina chase you to this bush. I must get to the melon bed, and if I went there now she'd see me."

Darzee was a featherbrained little fellow who could never hold more than one idea at a time in his head; and just because he knew that Nagaina's children were born in eggs like his own, he didn't think at first that it was fair to kill them. But his wife was a sensible bird, so she flew off from the nest, and left Darzee to keep the babies warm, and continue his song about the death of Nag.

She fluttered in front of Nagaina by the rubbish heap, and cried out: "Oh, my wing is broken! The boy in the house threw a stone at me and broke it." Then she fluttered more desperately than ever.

Nagaina lifted up her head and hissed: "You warned Rikki-tikki when I would have killed him. Indeed and truly, you've chosen a bad place to be lame in." And she moved toward Darzee's wife.

"The boy broke it with a stone!" shrieked Darzee's wife.

"Well, it may be some consolation to you when you're dead to know that I shall settle accounts with the boy. What is the use of running away? Little fool, look at me!"

Darzee's wife knew better than to do *that*, for a bird who looks at a snake's eyes gets so frightened that she cannot move. Darzee's wife fluttered on, piping sorrowfully and never leaving the ground, and Nagaina quickened her pace.

Rikki-tikki heard them going up the path from the stables, and he raced for the melon patch. There, in the warm litter about the melons, very cunningly hidden, he found twenty-five eggs, about the size of a bantam's eggs, but with whitish skin instead of shell.

"I was not a day too soon," he said; for he could see the baby cobras curled up inside the skin, and he knew that the minute they were hatched they could each kill a man or a mongoose. He bit off the tops of the eggs as fast as he could, taking care to crush the young cobras, and turned over the litter from time to time to see whether he had missed any.

At last there were only three eggs left, and Rikki-tikki began to chuckle to himself, when he heard Darzee's wife screaming: "Rikki-tikki, I led Nagaina toward the house, and she has gone into the veranda, and—oh, come quickly—she means killing!"

Rikki-tikki smashed two eggs, and tumbled backward down the melon bed with the third egg in his mouth, and scuttled to the veranda as hard as he could. Teddy and his mother and father were there at early breakfast, but they were not eating anything. They sat stone-still, and their faces were white. Nagaina was coiled up on the matting by Teddy's chair, within easy striking distance of Teddy's bare leg, and she was swaying to and fro singing a song of triumph.

"Son of the big man that killed Nag," she hissed, "stay still. I am not ready yet. Keep very still, all you three. If you move I strike, and if you do not move I strike. Oh, foolish people, who killed my Nag!"

Teddy's eyes were fixed on his father, and all his father could do was to whisper: "Sit still, Teddy. You mustn't move."

Then Rikki-tikki came up and cried: "Turn round, Nagaina; turn and fight!"

"All in good time," said she, without moving her eyes. "I will settle my account with *you* presently. Look at your friends, Rikki-tikki. They are afraid. If you come a step nearer I strike."

"Look at your eggs," said Rikki-tikki, "in the melon bed near the wall. Go and look, Nagaina."

The big snake turned half round, and saw the egg on the veranda. "Ah-h! Give it to me," she said.

Rikki-tikki put his paws one on each side of the egg, and his eyes were blood-red. "What price for a snake's egg? For a young king cobra? For the last—the very last of the brood? The ants are eating all the others down by the melon bed."

Nagaina spun clear round, forgetting everything for the sake of the one egg; and Rikki-tikki saw Teddy's father shoot out a big hand and drag Teddy across the little table with the teacups, out of reach of Nagaina.

"Tricked! Tricked! *Rikk-tck-tck!*" chuckled Rikki-tikki. "The boy is safe, and it was I—I—I that caught Nag by the hood last night in the bathroom." Then he began to jump up and down, all four feet together. "He threw me to and fro, but he could not shake me off. He was dead before the big man blew him in two. I did it. Come then, Nagaina, and fight with me. You shall not be a widow long."

Nagaina saw that she had lost her chance of killing Teddy, and the egg lay between Rikki-tikki's paws. "Give me the egg, and I will go away and never come back," she said, lowering her hood.

"Yes, you will go away, and you will never come back; for you will go to the rubbish heap with Nag. Fight, widow! The big man has gone for his gun! Fight!"

Rikki-tikki was bounding all round Nagaina, keeping just out of reach, his little eyes like hot coals. Nagaina gathered herself together, and flung out at him. Rikki-tikki jumped up and backward. Again and again and again she struck, and each time her head came with a whack on the matting of the veranda, and she gathered herself together like a watch spring. Then Rikki-tikki danced in a circle to get behind her, and Nagaina spun round to keep her head to his head, so that the rustle of her tail on the matting sounded like dry leaves blown along by the wind.

He had forgotten the egg. It still lay on the veranda, and Nagaina came nearer and nearer to it, till at last, while Rikki-tikki was drawing breath, she caught it in her mouth, turned to the veranda steps, and flew like an arrow down the path, with Rikki-tikki behind her. When the cobra runs for her life, she goes like a whiplash flicked across a horse's neck.

She headed straight for the long grass by the thornbush, and Rikki-tikki heard Darzee still singing his foolish little song of triumph. But Darzee's wife was wiser. She flew off her nest and flapped her wings about Nagaina's head. If Darzee had helped they might have turned her; but Nagaina only lowered her hood and went on. Still, the instant's delay brought Rikki-tikki up to her, and as she plunged into the rathole where she and Nag used to live, his little white teeth were clenched on her tail, and he went down with her—and very few mongooses care to follow a cobra into its hole. It was dark in the hole; and Rikki-tikki never knew when it might open out and give Nagaina room to turn and strike at him. He held on savagely, and struck out his feet to act as brakes on the dark slope of the hot, moist earth.

Then the grass by the mouth of the hole stopped waving, and Darzee said: "It is all over with Rikki-tikki! We must sing his death song. Valiant Rikki-tikki is dead! For Nagaina will surely kill him underground."

So he sang a very mournful song that he made up on the spur

of the minute, and just as he got to the most touching part the grass quivered again, and Rikki-tikki, covered with dirt, dragged himself out of the hole leg by leg, licking his whiskers. Darzee stopped with a little shout. Rikki-tikki shook some of the dust out of his fur and sneezed. "It is all over," he said. "The widow will never come out again." And the red ants that live between the grass stems heard him, and began to troop down, one after another, to see if he had spoken the truth.

Rikki-tikki curled himself up in the grass and slept where he was—slept and slept till it was late in the afternoon, for he had done a hard day's work.

"Now," he said, when he awoke, "I will go back to the house. Tell the Coppersmith, Darzee, and he will tell the garden that Nagaina is dead."

The Coppersmith is a bird who makes a noise exactly like the beating of a little hammer on a copper pot; he is the town crier to every Indian garden. As Rikki-tikki went up the path, he heard his "attention" notes like a tiny dinner gong; and then the steady "*Ding-dong-tock!* Nag is dead—*dong!* Nagaina is dead! *Ding-dong-tock!*" That set all the birds singing, and the frogs croaking; for Nag and Nagaina used to eat frogs as well as little birds.

When Rikki got to the house, Teddy and Teddy's mother and Teddy's father came out and almost cried over him; and that night he ate all that was given him till he could eat no more, and went to bed on Teddy's shoulder, where Teddy's mother saw him when she came to look late at night.

"He saved our lives and Teddy's life," she said to her husband. "Just think, he saved all our lives!"

Rikki-tikki woke up with a jump, for all the mongooses are light sleepers.

"Oh, it's you," said he. "What are you bothering for? All the cobras are dead; and if they weren't, I'm here."

Rikki-tikki had a right to be proud of himself; but he did not grow too proud, and he kept that garden as a mongoose should keep it, with tooth and jump and spring and bite, till never a cobra dared show its head inside the walls.

ALA NAG, which means Black Snake, had served the Indian Government in every way that an elephant could serve it for forty-seven years, and as he was fully twenty years old when he was caught, that makes him nearly seventy—a ripe age for an elephant. He remembered pushing, with a big leather pad on his forehead, at a gun stuck in deep mud, and that was before the Afghan War of 1842, and he had not then come to his full strength. His mother, Radha Pyari—Radha the darling—who had been caught in the same drive with Kala Nag, told him, before his little milk tusks had dropped out, that elephants who were afraid always got hurt; and Kala Nag knew that that advice was good, for the first time that he saw a shell burst he backed, screaming, into a stand of piled rifles, and the bayonets pricked him in all his softest places. So before he was twenty-five he gave up being afraid, and so he was the best-loved and the best-looked-after elephant in the service of the Government of India. He had carried twelve hundred pounds' weight of tents on the march in Upper India; he had been hoisted into a ship at the end of a steam crane and taken for days across the water, and made to carry a mortar on his back in a strange and rocky country very far from India, and had come back again entitled, so the soldiers said, to the Abyssinian War Medal. Afterward he had been sent down thousands of miles south to haul and pile big balks of teak in the timberyards at Moulmein. There he had half killed an insubordinate young elephant who was shirking his fair share of the work.

After that he was taken off timber-hauling, and employed, with a few score other elephants who were trained in the business, in helping to catch wild elephants among the Garo Hills. Elephants are very strictly preserved by the Indian Government. There is one whole department which does nothing else but hunt them, and catch them, and break them in, and send them up and down the country as they are needed for work.

Kala Nag stood ten feet at the shoulders, and his tusks had been cut off short at five feet, and bound round the ends, to prevent them splitting, with bands of copper; but he could do more with those stumps than any untrained elephant could do with the real sharpened ones.

When, after weeks of cautious driving of scattered elephants across the hills, the forty or fifty wild monsters were driven into the last stockade, and the big drop-gate, made of tree trunks lashed together, jarred down behind them, Kala Nag, at the word of command, would go into that flaring, trumpeting pandemonium (generally at night, when the flicker of the torches made it difficult to judge distances), and, picking out the biggest and wildest tusker of the mob, would hammer him and hustle him into quiet while the men on the backs of the other elephants roped and tied the smaller ones.

There was nothing in the way of fighting that Kala Nag, the old wise Black Snake, did not know, for he had stood up more than once in his time to the charge of the wounded tiger, and, curling up his soft trunk to be out of harm's way, had knocked the springing brute sideways in midair with a quick sickle-cut of his head; had knocked him over, and kneeled upon him with his huge knees till the life went out with a gasp and a howl, and there was only a fluffy striped thing on the ground.

"Yes," said Big Toomai, his driver, the son of Black Toomai who had taken him to Abyssinia, and grandson of Toomai of the Elephants who had seen him caught, "there is nothing that the Black Snake fears except me."

"He is afraid of *me* also," said Little Toomai, standing up to his full height of four feet, with only one rag upon him. He was ten years old, the eldest son of Big Toomai, and, according to custom, he would take his father's place on Kala Nag's neck when he grew up, and would handle the heavy iron ankus, the elephant goad that had been worn smooth by his father, and his grandfather, and his great-grandfather. He knew what he was talking of; for he had been born under Kala Nag's shadow, had played with the end of his trunk before he could walk, had taken him down to water as soon as he could walk, and Kala Nag would no more have dreamed of disobeying his shrill little orders than he would have dreamed of killing him on that day when Big Toomai carried the little brown baby under Kala Nag's tusks, and told him to salute his master that was to be.

"Yes," said Little Toomai, "he is afraid of *me*," and he took long strides up to Kala Nag, called him a fat old pig, and made him lift up his feet one after the other.

"Wah!" said Little Toomai, "thou art a big elephant," and he wagged his fluffy head. "When thou art old, Kala Nag, there will come some rich Rajah, and he will buy thee from the Government, on account of thy size and thy manners, and then thou wilt have nothing to do but to carry gold earrings in thy ears, and a gold howdah on thy back, and a red cloth covered with gold on thy sides, and walk at the head of the processions of the King. Then I shall sit on thy neck, with a silver ankus, and men will run before us with golden sticks, crying, 'Room for the King's elephant!' That will be good, Kala Nag, but not so good as this hunting in the jungles."

"Umph!" said Big Toomai. "Thou art as wild as a buffalo-calf. This running up and down among the hills is not the best Government service. I am getting old, and I do not love wild elephants. Give me brick elephant lines, one stall to each elephant, and flat, broad roads to exercise upon, instead of this come-and-go camping. Aha, the Cawnpore barracks were good. There was a bazaar close by and only three hours' work a day."

Little Toomai remembered the Cawnpore elephant lines and said nothing. He very much preferred this camp life, and hated those broad, flat roads. What he liked was the scramble up bridle paths that only an elephant could take; the glimpses of the wild elephants browsing miles away; the rush of the frightened pig and peacock under Kala Nag's feet; the beautiful misty mornings when nobody knew where they would camp that night; the steady, cautious drive of the wild elephants, and the mad rush and hulla-baloo of the last night's drive, when the elephants poured into the stockade like boulders in a landslide, found that they could not get out, and flung themselves at the heavy posts only to be driven back by yells and flaring torches and volleys of blank cartridges. Little Toomai would wave his torch and yell with the best.

The really good time came when the driving out began, and the Keddah—that is, the stockade—looked like a picture of the end of the world, and men had to make signs to one another, because they could not hear themselves speak. Then Little Toomai would climb up to the top of one of the quivering stockade posts, his sun-bleached brown hair flying loose all over his shoulders, and as soon as there was a lull you could hear his high-pitched yells of encouragement to Kala Nag, above the trumpeting and crashing, and snapping of ropes, and groans of the tethered elephants. "*Somalo! Somalo!* [Careful! Careful!] *Maro! Maro!* [Hit him! Hit him!] *Hai! Yai! Kya-a-ah!*" he would shout, and the big fight between Kala Nag and the wild elephant would sway to and fro across the Keddah, and the old elephant-catchers would wipe the sweat out of their eyes, and nod to Little Toomai wriggling with joy on the top of the posts.

He did more than wriggle. One night he slid down from the post and slipped in between the elephants, and threw up the loose end of a rope, which had dropped, to a driver who was trying to get a purchase on the leg of a kicking young calf. Kala Nag saw him, caught him in his trunk, and handed him up to Big Toomai, who slapped him then and there, and put him back on the post.

Next morning he gave him a scolding, and said: "Are not good brick elephant lines and a little tent-carrying enough, that thou must needs go elephant-catching on thy own account, little worthless? Now those foolish hunters have spoken to Petersen Sahib of the matter." Little Toomai was frightened. He did not know much of white men, but Petersen Sahib was the greatest white man in the world to him. He was the head of all the Keddah operations—the man who caught all the elephants for the Government of India, and who knew more about the ways of elephants than any living man.

"What will happen?" said Little Toomai.

"Happen! The worst that can happen. Petersen Sahib is a madman. Else why should he go hunting these wild devils? He may even require thee to be an elephant-catcher, to sleep anywhere in these fever-filled jungles, and at last to be trampled to death in the Keddah. Next week the catching is over, and we of the plains— mahouts, not mere hunters—are sent back to our stations. Bad one! Wicked one! Worthless son! Go and wash Kala Nag and attend to his ears, and see that there are no thorns in his feet; or else Petersen Sahib will surely catch thee and make thee a wild hunter. Bah! Shame! Go!"

Little Toomai went off without saying a word, but he told Kala Nag all his grievances while he was examining his feet. "No matter," said Little Toomai, turning up the fringe of Kala Nag's huge right ear. "They have said my name to Petersen Sahib, and perhaps—and perhaps—and perhaps—who knows? Hai! That is a big thorn that I have pulled out!"

The next few days were spent in walking the newly caught wild elephants up and down between a couple of tame ones to prevent them from giving too much trouble on the downward march to the plains, and in taking stock of the blankets and ropes and things that had been worn out or lost in the forest.

Petersen Sahib came in on his clever she-elephant Pudmini. He had been paying off other camps among the hills, and there was a native clerk sitting at a table under a tree to pay the drivers their wages. As each man was paid he went back to his elephant, and joined the line that stood ready to start. The catchers, and hunters, and beaters, the men of the regular Keddah, who stayed in the jungle year in and year out, sat on the backs of the elephants that belonged to Petersen Sahib's permanent force and made fun of the drivers who were going away, and laughed when the newly caught elephants broke the line and ran about.

Big Toomai went up to the clerk with Little Toomai behind

him, and Machua Appa, the head tracker, said in an undertone to a friend of his, "There goes one piece of good elephant-stuff at least. 'Tis a pity to send that young jungle cock to molt in the plains."

Now Petersen Sahib had ears all over him, as a man must have who listens to the most silent of all living things—the wild elephant. He turned where he was lying along Pudmini's back, and said, "What is that? I did not know of a man among the plains-drivers who had wit enough to rope even a dead elephant."

"This is not a man, but a boy. He went into the Keddah at the last drive, and threw Barmao there the rope when we were trying to get that young calf with the blotch on his shoulder away from his mother."

Machua Appa pointed at Little Toomai, and Petersen Sahib looked, and Little Toomai bowed to the earth.

"He throw a rope? He is smaller than a picket pin. Little one, what is thy name?" said Petersen Sahib.

Little Toomai was too frightened to speak, but Kala Nag was behind him, and Toomai made a sign with his hand, and the elephant caught him up in his trunk and held him level with Pudmini's forehead, in front of the great Petersen Sahib. Then Little Toomai covered his face with his hands, for, except where elephants were concerned, he was just as bashful as a child could be.

"Oho!" said Petersen Sahib, smiling underneath his mustache, "and why didst thou teach thy elephant *that* trick? Was it to help thee steal green corn from the roofs of the houses when the ears are put out to dry?"

"Not green corn, Protector of the Poor—melons," said Little Toomai, and all the men sitting about broke into a roar of laughter. Most of them had taught their elephants that trick when they were boys. Little Toomai was hanging eight feet up in the air, and he wished very much that he were eight feet underground.

"He is Toomai, my son, Sahib," said Big Toomai, scowling. "He is a very bad boy, and he will end in a jail, Sahib."

"Of that I have my doubts," said Petersen Sahib. "A boy who can face a full Keddah at his age does not end in jails. See, little one, here are four annas to spend on sweetmeats because thou hast a little head under that great thatch of hair. In time thou mayest become a hunter too." Big Toomai scowled more than ever. "Remember, though, that Keddahs are not good for children to play in," Petersen Sahib went on.

"Must I never go there, Sahib?" asked Little Toomai, with a big gasp.

"Yes." Petersen Sahib smiled again. "When thou hast seen the elephants dance. Come to me when thou hast seen the elephants dance, and then I will let thee go into all the Keddahs."

There was another roar of laughter, for that is an old joke among elephant-catchers, and it means just never. There are great cleared flat places hidden away in the forests that are called elephants' ballrooms, but even these are only found by accident, and no man has ever seen the elephants dance. When a driver boasts of his skill and bravery the other drivers say, "And when didst *thou* see the elephants dance?"

Kala Nag put Little Toomai down, and he bowed to the earth again and went away with his father, and gave the silver four-anna piece to his mother, who was nursing his baby brother, and they all were put up on Kala Nag's back, and the line of grunting, squealing elephants rolled down the hill path to the plains. It was a very lively march on account of the new elephants, who needed coaxing or beating every other minute.

Big Toomai prodded Kala Nag spitefully, for he was very angry, but Little Toomai was too happy to speak. Petersen Sahib had noticed him, so he felt as a private soldier would feel if he had been called out of the ranks and praised by his commander in chief.

"What did Petersen Sahib mean by the elephant dance?" he said at last.

Big Toomai grunted. "That thou shouldst never be one of these hill buffaloes of trackers. *That* was what he meant. Oh, you in front, what is blocking the way?"

An Assamese driver, two or three elephants ahead, turned round angrily, crying: "Bring up Kala Nag and knock this youngster of mine into good behavior. Why should Petersen Sahib have chosen *me* to go down with you donkeys of the rice fields? Lay your beast alongside, Toomai, and let him prod with his tusks. By all the gods of the Hills, these new elephants are possessed, or else they can smell their companions in the jungle."

Kala Nag hit the new elephant in the ribs and knocked the wind out of him, as Big Toomai said, "We have swept the hills of wild elephants at the last catch. It is only your carelessness in driving."

"Hear him!" said the other driver. "*We* have swept the hills! Ho! ho! You are very wise, you plains people. Anyone but a mud-head who never saw the jungle would know that *they* know that the drives are ended for the season. Therefore all the wild elephants tonight will—but why should I waste wisdom on a river turtle?"

"What will they do?" Little Toomai called out.

"*Ohé*, little one. Art thou there? Well, I will tell thee, for thou hast a cool head. They will dance, and it behooves thy father, who has swept *all* the hills of *all* the elephants, to double-chain his pickets tonight."

"What talk is this?" said Big Toomai. "For forty years, father and son, we have tended elephants, and we have never heard such moonshine about dances."

"Well, leave thy elephants unshackled tonight and see what comes; as for their dancing, I have seen the place where— *Bapree-Bap!* How many windings has the Dihang River? Here is another ford, and we must swim the calves."

And in this way, talking and wrangling and splashing through the rivers, they made their first march to a sort of receiving camp for the new elephants.

Then the elephants were chained by their hind legs to their big stumps of pickets, and extra ropes were fitted to the new elephants, and the fodder was piled before them, and the hill-drivers went back to Petersen Sahib through the afternoon light, telling the plains-drivers to be extra careful that night, and laughing when they were asked the reason.

Little Toomai attended to Kala Nag's supper, and as evening fell, wandered through the camp, unspeakably happy, in search of a tom-tom. When an Indian child's heart is full, he does not run about and make a noise in an irregular fashion. He sits down to a sort of revel all by himself. And Little Toomai had been spoken to by Petersen Sahib! The sweetmeat-seller in the camp lent him a little tom-tom—a drum beaten with the flat of the hand—and he sat down, cross-legged, before Kala Nag as the stars began to come out, the tom-tom in his lap, and he thumped and he thumped and he thumped, and the more he thought of the great honor that had been done to him, the more he thumped. There was no tune and no words, but the thumping made him happy.

The new elephants strained at their ropes, and squealed and trumpeted from time to time, and he could hear his mother in the camp hut putting his small brother to sleep with an old, old song about the great God Shiv. It is a very soothing lullaby, and the first verse says:

> Shiv, who poured the harvest and made the winds to blow,
> Sitting at the doorways of a day of long ago,
> Gave to each his portion, food and toil and fate,
> From the King upon the guddee to the Beggar at the gate.
> All things made he—Shiva the Preserver.
> Mahadeo! Mahadeo! He made all—
> Thorn for the camel, fodder for the kine,
> And mother's heart for sleepy head, O little son of mine!

Little Toomai came in with a joyous *tunk-a-tunk* at the end of each verse, till he felt sleepy and stretched himself on the fodder at Kala Nag's side.

At last the elephants began to lie down one after another, till only Kala Nag was left standing up; and he rocked slowly from side to side, his ears put forward to listen to the night wind as it blew very slowly across the hills. The air was full of all the night noises that, taken together, make one big silence—the click of one bamboo stem against the other, the rustle of something alive in the undergrowth, the scratch and squawk of a half-waked bird, and the fall of water ever so far away. Little Toomai slept for some time, and when he waked it was brilliant moonlight, and Kala Nag was still standing up with his ears cocked. Little Toomai turned, rustling in the fodder, and watched the curve of his big back against half the stars in heaven; and while he watched he heard, so far away that it sounded no more than a pinhole of noise pricked through the stillness, the "hoot-toot" of a wild elephant.

All the elephants in the lines jumped up as if they had been shot, and their grunts at last waked the sleeping mahouts, and they came out and drove in the picket pegs with big mallets, and tightened this rope and knotted that till all was quiet. One new elephant had nearly grubbed up his picket, and Big Toomai took off Kala Nag's leg chain and shackled that elephant fore foot to hind foot, but slipped a loop of grass string round Kala Nag's leg, and told him to remember that he was tied fast. He knew that he and his father and his grandfather had done the very same thing hundreds of times before. Kala Nag did not answer to the order by gurgling, as he usually did. He stood still, looking out across the moonlight, his ears spread like fans, up to the great folds of the Garo Hills.

"Look to him if he grows restless in the night," said Big Toomai to Little Toomai, and he went into the hut and slept. Little Toomai was just going to sleep, too, when he heard the coir string snap with a little "tang," and Kala Nag rolled out of his pickets as slowly and as silently as a cloud rolls out of the mouth of a valley. Little Toomai pattered after him, barefooted, down the road in the moonlight, calling under his breath, "Kala Nag! Kala Nag! Take me with you, O Kala Nag!" The elephant turned without a sound, took three strides back to the boy in the moonlight, put down his trunk, swung him up to his neck, and almost before Little Toomai had settled his knees, slipped into the forest.

There was one blast of furious trumpeting from the lines, and then the silence shut down on everything, and Kala Nag began to move. Sometimes a tuft of high grass washed along his sides as a wave washes along the sides of a ship, and sometimes a bamboo would creak where his shoulder touched it; but between those times he moved without any sound, drifting through the thick Garo forest as though it had been smoke. He was going uphill, but Little Toomai could not tell in what direction.

Then Kala Nag reached the crest of the ascent and stopped for a minute, and Little Toomai could see the tops of the trees lying all speckled and furry under the moonlight for miles and miles, and the blue-white mist over the river in the hollow. Toomai leaned forward and looked, and he felt that the forest was awake below him—awake and crowded. A big fruit-eating bat brushed past his ear; a porcupine's quills rattled in the thicket; and in the darkness between the tree stems he heard a hog-bear snuffing and digging hard in the moist, warm earth.

Then the branches closed over his head again, and Kala Nag began to go slowly down into the valley—not quietly this time, but in one rush. The huge limbs moved as steadily as pistons, eight feet to each stride. The undergrowth on either side of him ripped with a noise like torn canvas, and the saplings that he heaved away right and left with his shoulders sprang back again, and banged him on the flank, and great trails of creepers, all matted together, hung from his tusks as he threw his head from side to side and plowed out his pathway. Then Little Toomai laid himself down close to the great neck, lest a swinging bough should sweep him to the ground, and he wished that he were back in the lines again.

The grass began to get squashy, and Kala Nag's feet sucked and squelched as he put them down, and the night mist at the bottom of the valley chilled Little Toomai. There was a splash and a trample, and the rush of running water, and Kala Nag strode through the bed of a river. Above the noise of the water Little Toomai could hear more splashing and some trumpeting both upstream and down—great grunts and angry snortings, and all the mist about him seemed to be full of rolling, wavy shadows.

"*Ai!*" he said, half aloud, his teeth chattering. "The elephant-folk are out tonight. It *is* the dance, then."

Kala Nag swashed out of the water, blew his trunk clear, and began another climb; but this time he was not alone, and the path was made already, six feet wide, in front of him. Many elephants must have gone that way only a few minutes before. Little Toomai looked back, and behind him a great wild tusker, with his little pig's eyes glowing like hot coals, was just lifting himself out of the misty river. Then the trees closed up again, and they went on, with trumpetings and crashings.

At last Kala Nag stood still between two tree trunks at the very top of the hill. They were part of a circle of trees that grew round an irregular space of some three or four acres, and in all that space the ground had been trampled down as hard as a brick floor.

The moonlight showed it all iron gray, except where some elephants stood upon it, and their shadows were inky black. Little Toomai looked, holding his breath, with his eyes starting out of his head, and as he looked, more and more and more elephants swung out into the open from between the tree trunks. Little Toomai could count only up to ten, and he counted again and again on his fingers till he lost count of the tens, and his head began to swim.

There were white-tusked wild males, with fallen leaves and nuts and twigs lying in the wrinkles of their necks and the folds of their ears; fat, slow-footed she-elephants, with restless little pinky-black calves only three or four feet high running under their stomachs; savage old bull-elephants, scarred from shoulder to flank with great weals and cuts of bygone fights, and the caked dirt of their solitary mud baths dropping from their shoulders; and there was one with a broken tusk and the marks of the full-stroke, the terrible drawing scrape of a tiger's claws, on his side.

They were standing head to head, or walking to and fro across the ground in couples, or rocking and swaying all by themselves—scores and scores of elephants.

Toomai knew that so long as he lay still on Kala Nag's neck nothing would happen to him; for even in the rush and scramble of a Keddah-drive a wild elephant does not reach up with his trunk and drag a man off the neck of a tame elephant; and these elephants were not thinking of men that night. Once they started and put their ears forward when they heard the chinking of a leg iron in the forest, but it was Pudmini, Petersen Sahib's pet elephant, her chain snapped short off, grunting up the hillside. She must have broken her pickets, and come straight from Petersen Sahib's camp.

At last there was no sound of any more elephants moving in the forest, and Kala Nag rolled out from his station between the trees and went into the middle of the crowd, clucking and gurgling, and all the elephants began to talk in their own tongue, and to move about.

Still lying down, Little Toomai looked down upon scores and scores of broad backs, and wagging ears, and tossing trunks, and little rolling eyes. He heard the click of tusks as they crossed other tusks by accident, and the dry rustle of trunks twined together, and the chafing of enormous sides and shoulders in the crowd, and the incessant flick and *hissh* of the great tails. Then a cloud came over the moon, and he sat in black darkness; but the quiet, steady pushing and gurgling went on just the same. He knew that there were elephants all round Kala Nag, and that there was no chance of backing him out of the assembly; so he set his teeth and shivered. In a Keddah at least there was torchlight and shouting, but here he was all alone in the dark, and once a trunk came up and touched him on the knee.

Then an elephant trumpeted, and they all took it up for five or ten terrible seconds. The dew from the trees above spattered down like rain on the unseen backs, and a dull booming noise began, not very loud at first, and Little Toomai could not tell what it was; but it grew and grew, and Kala Nag lifted up one forefoot and then the other, and brought them down on the ground, one—two, one—two, as steadily as trip-hammers. The elephants were stamping all together now, and it sounded like a war drum beaten at the mouth of a cave. The ground rocked and shivered, and Little Toomai put his hands up to his ears to shut out the sound. But it was all one gigantic jar that ran through him—this stamp of hundreds of heavy feet on the raw earth. Once or twice he could feel Kala Nag and all the others surge forward a few strides, and the thumping would change to the crushing sound of juicy green things being bruised, but in a minute or two the boom of feet on hard earth began again. A tree was creaking and groaning somewhere near him. He put out his arm and felt the bark, but Kala Nag moved forward, still tramping, and he could not tell where he was in the clearing. The booming must have lasted fully two hours, and Little Toomai ached in every nerve; but he knew by the smell of the night air that the dawn was coming.

The morning broke in one sheet of pale yellow behind the green hills, and the booming stopped with the first ray, as though the light had been an order. Before Little Toomai had got the ringing out of his head, before even he had shifted his position, there was not an elephant in sight except Kala Nag and Pudmini, and there was neither sign nor rustle nor whisper down the hillsides to show where the others had gone.

Little Toomai stared again and again. The clearing, as he remembered it, had grown in the night. The undergrowth and the jungle grass at the sides had been rolled back. Now Little Toomai understood the trampling. The elephants had stamped out more room—had stamped the thick grass and juicy cane to trash, the trash into slivers, the slivers into tiny fibers, and the fibers into hard earth.

"Wah!" said Little Toomai, and his eyes were very heavy. "Kala Nag, my lord, let us keep by Pudmini and go to Petersen Sahib's camp, or I shall drop from thy neck."

Two hours later, as Petersen Sahib was eating early breakfast, the elephants, who had been double-chained that night, began to trumpet, and Pudmini, mired to the shoulders, with Kala Nag, very footsore, shambled into the camp.

Little Toomai's face was gray and pinched, and his hair was full of leaves and drenched with dew; but he tried to salute Petersen Sahib, and cried faintly: "The dance—the elephant dance! I have seen it, and—I die!" As Kala Nag sat down, he slid off his neck in a dead faint.

In two hours he was lying very contentedly in Petersen Sahib's hammock with Petersen Sahib's shooting coat under his head, and a glass of warm milk, a little brandy, with a dash of quinine, inside of him; and while the old hairy, scarred hunters of the jungles sat three-deep before him, looking at him as though he were a spirit, he told his tale in short words, as a child will, and wound up with: "Now, if I lie in one word, send men to see, and they will find that the elephant-folk have trampled down more room in their dance-room, and they will find ten and ten, and many times ten, tracks leading to that dance-room. They made more room with their feet. Kala Nag took me, and I saw. Also Kala Nag is very leg-weary!"

Little Toomai lay back and slept all through the long afternoon and into the twilight, and while he slept Petersen Sahib and Machua Appa followed the track of the two elephants for fifteen miles across the hills. Petersen Sahib had spent eighteen years in catching elephants, and he had only once before found such a dance place, and Machua Appa had no need to look twice at the clearing to see what had been done there, or to scratch with his toe in the packed, rammed earth.

"The child speaks truth," said he. "All this was done last night, and I have counted seventy tracks crossing the river. See, Sahib, where Pudmini's leg iron cut the bark off that tree! Yes, she was here too."

They looked at each other, and up and down, and they wondered; for the ways of elephants are beyond the wit of any man, black or white, to fathom.

"Forty years and five," said Machua Appa, "have I followed my lord the elephant, but never have I heard that any child of man had seen what this child has seen. By all the gods of the Hills, it is—what can we say?" and he shook his head.

When they got back to camp it was time for the evening meal. Petersen Sahib ate alone in his tent, but he gave orders that the camp should have two sheep and some fowls, as well as a double ration of flour and rice and salt, for he knew that there would be a feast.

Big Toomai had come up hotfoot from the camp in the plains to search for his son and his elephant, and now that he had found them he looked at them as though he were afraid of them both. And there was a feast by the blazing campfires in front of the lines of picketed elephants, and Little Toomai was the hero of it all; and the big brown elephant-catchers, the trackers and drivers and ropers, the men who know all the secrets of breaking the wildest elephants, passed him from one to the other, and they marked his forehead with blood from the breast of a newly killed jungle cock, to show that he was initiated and free of all the jungles.

And at last, when the flames died down, and the red light of the logs made the elephants look as though they had been dipped in blood too, Machua Appa, the head of all the drivers of all the Keddahs—Machua Appa, who was so great that he had no other name than Machua Appa—leaped to his feet, with Little Toomai held high in the air above his head, and shouted: "Listen, my brothers. Listen, too, you my lords in the lines there, for I, Machua Appa, am speaking! This little one shall not more be called Little Toomai, but Toomai of the Elephants, as his great-grandfather was called before him. What never man has seen he has seen through the long night, and the favor of the elephant-folk and of the gods of the Jungles is with him. He shall become a great tracker; he shall become greater than I, even I—Machua Appa! He shall follow the new trail, and the stale trail, and the mixed trail, with a clear eye! He shall take no harm in the Keddah when he runs under their bellies to rope the wild tuskers; and if he slips before the feet of the charging bull-elephant, that bull-elephant shall know who he is and shall not crush him. *Aihai!* my lords in the chains"—he whirled up the line of pickets—"here is the little one that has seen your dances in your hidden places—the sight that never man saw! Give him honor, my lords! *Salaam karo*, my children! Make your salute to Toomai of the Elephants! Gunga Pershad, ahaa! Hira Guj, Birchi Guj, Kuttar Guj, ahaa! Pudmini—thou hast seen him at the dance, and thou too, Kala Nag, my pearl among elephants—ahaa! Together! To Toomai of the Elephants. *Barrao!*"

And at that last wild yell the whole line flung up their trunks till the tips touched their foreheads, and broke out into the full salute, the crashing trumpet-peal that only the Viceroy of India hears—the Salaamut of the Keddah.

But it was all for the sake of Little Toomai, who had seen what never man had seen before—the dance of the elephants at night and alone in the heart of the Garo Hills!

HERE was once a man in India who was Prime Minister of one of the semi-independent native States in the northwestern part of the country. He was a Brahmin, so high-caste that caste ceased to have any particular meaning for him; and his father had been an important official in an old-fashioned Hindu court. But as Purun Dass grew up he felt that the old order was changing, and that if anyone wished to get on in the world he must stand well with the English. At the same time a native official must keep his own master's favor. This was a difficult game, but the quiet, close-mouthed young Brahmin, helped by a good English education at a Bombay university, played it coolly, and rose to be Prime Minister of the kingdom. That is to say, he held more real power than the Maharajah.

When the old King—who was suspicious of the English, their railways and telegraphs—died, Purun Dass stood high with his young successor, who had been tutored by an Englishman; and between them they established schools for little girls, made roads, and started State dispensaries. The Prime Minister became the friend of Viceroys, and Governors, and medical missionaries, and hard-riding English officers, as well as of hosts of tourists.

At last he went to England on a visit. There he met and talked with everyone worth knowing, was given honorary degrees by learned universities, and saw a great deal more than he said. When he returned to India, the Viceroy made a special visit to confer upon the Maharajah the Grand Cross of the Star of India—all diamonds and ribbons and enamel; and at the same ceremony, Purun Dass was made a Knight Commander of the Order of the Indian Empire, so that his name stood Sir Purun Dass, K.C.I.E.

Next month he did a thing no Englishman would have dreamed

of doing; for, so far as the world's affairs went, he died. The priests knew what had happened, and the people guessed; but in India a man can do as he pleases and nobody asks why; and the fact that Sir Purun Dass, K.C.I.E., had taken up the begging bowl and ocher-colored dress of a Sannyasi, or holy man, was considered nothing extraordinary. He had been, as the Old Law recommends, twenty years a youth, twenty years a fighter—though he had never carried a weapon—and twenty years head of a household. He had used his wealth and power for what he knew both to be worth; he had taken honor when it came his way. Now he let those things go, as a man drops the cloak he no longer needs.

He walked through the city gates, an antelope skin and brass-handled crutch under his arm, and a begging bowl of polished brown *coco-de-mer* in his hand, barefoot, alone, with eyes cast on the ground. Purun Dass was a Sannyasi now—a houseless, wandering mendicant, depending on his neighbors for his daily bread; and so long as there is a morsel to divide in India, neither priest nor beggar starves. He had never in his life tasted meat, and very seldom eaten even fish. A five-pound note would have covered his personal expenses for food through any one of the many years in which he had been absolute master of millions of money. Even when he was being lionized in London he had held before him his dream of peace and quiet—the long, white, dusty Indian road, printed all over with bare feet, the incessant, slow-moving traffic, and the sharp-smelling woodsmoke curling up under the fig trees in the twilight, where the wayfarers sit at their evening meal.

At night Purun Dass spread his antelope skin where the darkness overtook him—sometimes in a Sannyasi monastery by the roadside; sometimes on the outskirts of a village, where the children would steal up with the food their parents had prepared. It was all one to Purun Dass—or Purun Bhagat, as he called himself now. But unconsciously his feet drew him northward and eastward to Kurnool; from Kurnool to ruined Samanah, and then along the dried bed of the Gugger River that fills only when the rain falls in the hills, till one day he saw the far line of the great Himalayas.

Then Purun Bhagat smiled, for he remembered that his mother

was a Hill-woman, always homesick for the snows—and that the least touch of Hill blood draws a man in the end back to where he belongs. "Yonder," said Purun Bhagat, breasting the lower slopes of the Siwaliks, "yonder I shall sit down and get knowledge"; and the cool wind of the Himalayas whistled about his ears as he trod the road that led to Simla and beyond.

That night he slept in an empty hut at Chota Simla, which looks like the last end of the earth, but it was only the beginning of his journey. He followed the Himalaya–Tibet road, the little ten-foot track that is blasted out of solid rock, or strutted out on timbers over gulfs a thousand feet deep; that dips into warm, wet, shut-in valleys, and climbs out across hill-shoulders where the sun strikes like a burning glass; or turns through dripping, dark forests where the tree ferns dress the trunks from head to heel, and the pheasant calls to his mate. And he met Tibetan herdsmen with their dogs and flocks of sheep, and wandering woodcutters, and cloaked and blanketed Lamas from Tibet; or else for a long, clear day he would see nothing more than a black bear grunting and rooting below in the valley. When he first started, the roar of the world he had left still rang in his ears, as the roar of a tunnel rings long after the train has passed through; but when he had put the Mutteeanee Pass behind him that was all done, and Purun Bhagat was alone with himself, walking, wondering, and thinking, his eyes on the ground, and his thoughts with the clouds.

One evening he crossed the highest pass he had met till then— it had been a two-day climb—and came out on a line of snowpeaks that banded all the horizon—mountains from fifteen to twenty thousand feet high, looking almost near enough to hit with a stone, though they were fifty or sixty miles away. The pass was crowned with dense, dark forest—walnut, wild cherry, and wild pear, but mostly deodar, which is the Himalayan cedar; and under the shadow of the deodars stood a deserted shrine to Kali, who is sometimes worshiped against the smallpox.

Purun Dass swept the stone floor clean, smiled at the grinning statue, made himself a little mud fireplace, spread his antelope skin on a bed of fresh pine needles, and sat down to rest.

Immediately below him the hillside fell away, clean and cleared for fifteen hundred feet, where a little village of stone-walled houses, with roofs of beaten earth, clung to the steep tilt. All round it the tiny terraced fields lay out like aprons of patchwork on the knees of the mountain, and cows no bigger than beetles grazed between the smooth stone circles of the threshing floors. Looking across the valley, the eye was deceived by the size of things, and could not at first realize that what seemed to be low scrub, on the opposite mountain-flank, was in truth a forest of hundred-foot pines. Purun Bhagat saw an eagle swoop across the gigantic hollow, but the great bird dwindled to a dot ere it was halfway over. And "Here shall I find peace," said Purun Bhagat.

Now, a Hill-man makes nothing of a few hundred feet up or down, and as soon as the villagers saw the smoke in the deserted shrine, the village priest climbed up the terraced hillside to welcome the stranger. When he met Purun Bhagat's eyes—the eyes of a man used to controlling thousands—he bowed to the earth, took the polished brown begging bowl without a word, and returned to the village saying, "We have at last a holy man. Never have I seen such a man. He is of the Plains—a Brahmin of the Brahmins." Then all the housewives of the village said, "Think you he will stay with us?" and each did her best to cook the most savory meal for the Bhagat. Hill food is very simple, but with buckwheat and Indian corn, and rice and red pepper, and little fish out of the stream, and honey from the fluelike hives built in the stone walls, and dried apricots, and turmeric, and wild ginger, a devout woman can make good things, and it was a full bowl that the priest carried to the Bhagat. Was he going to stay? asked the priest. Had he a blanket against the cold weather? Was the food good?

Purun Bhagat ate, and thanked the giver. It was in his mind to stay. That was sufficient, said the priest. Let the begging bowl be placed outside the shrine, in the hollow made by those two twisted roots, and daily should the Bhagat be fed; for the village felt honored that such a man should tarry among them.

That day saw the end of Purun Bhagat's wanderings. He had come to the place appointed for him—the silence and the space.

After this, time stopped, and he, sitting at the mouth of the shrine, could not tell whether he were alive or dead; a man with control of his limbs, or a part of the hills, and the clouds, and the shifting rain and sunlight. He would repeat a Name softly to himself a hundred hundred times, till, at each repetition, he seemed to move more out of his body, sweeping up to the doors of some tremendous discovery; but, just as the door was opening, his body would drag him back, and, with grief, he felt he was locked up again in the flesh and bones of Purun Bhagat.

Every morning the filled begging bowl was laid silently in the crutch of the roots outside the shrine. Sometimes the priest brought it; sometimes a Ladakhi trader, lodging in the village, and anxious to get merit, trudged up the path; but, more often, it was the woman who had cooked the meal overnight; and she would murmur, hardly above her breath: "Speak for me before the gods, Bhagat. Speak for such a one, the wife of so-and-so!" Now and then some bold child would be allowed the honor, and Purun Bhagat would hear him drop the bowl and run as fast as his little legs could carry him, but the Bhagat never came down to the village. It was laid out like a map at his feet. He could see the evening gatherings, held on the circle of the threshing floors; could see the wonderful green of the young rice, the indigo blues of the Indian corn and, in its season, the red bloom of the amaranth.

When the year turned, the roofs of the huts were all little squares of purest gold, for it was on the roofs that they laid out their cobs of corn to dry. Hiving and harvest, rice-sowing and husking, passed before his eyes, all embroidered down there on the many-sided plots of fields, and he thought of them all, and wondered what they all led to at the long last.

Even in populated India a man cannot a day sit still before the wild things run over him as though he were a rock; and in that wilderness very soon the wild things, who knew Kali's Shrine well, came back to look at the intruder. The langurs, big gray-whiskered monkeys, were the first, for they are alive with curiosity; and when they had upset the begging bowl, and rolled it round the floor, and tried their teeth on the brass-handled crutch, they decided that the human being who sat so still was harmless. At evening, they would leap down from the pines and beg with their hands for things to eat, and then swing off in graceful curves. They liked the warmth of the fire, too, and huddled round it till Purun Bhagat had to push them aside to throw on more fuel; and in the morning he would often find a furry ape sharing his blanket.

Then came the barasingh, a big deer. He wished to rub off the velvet of his horns against the cold stones of Kali's statue, and stamped his feet when he saw the man at the shrine. But Purun Bhagat never moved, and, little by little, the royal stag edged up and nuzzled his shoulder. Purun Bhagat slid one cool hand along the hot antlers, and the touch soothed the fretted beast, who bowed his head, and Purun Bhagat very softly rubbed off the velvet. Afterward, the barasingh brought his doe and fawn, or would come alone at night, his eyes green in the fire-flicker, to take his share of fresh walnuts. At last the musk deer, the shyest of the deerlets, came, too, her big rabbity ears erect. Purun Bhagat called them all "my brothers," and his low call of "*Bhai! Bhai!*" would draw them from the forest at noon if they were within earshot. The Himalayan black bear, moody and suspicious—Sona, who has the V-shaped white mark under his chin—passed that way more than once; and since the Bhagat showed no fear, Sona showed no anger, but watched him, and came closer, and begged a share of the caresses, and a dole of bread or wild berries.

Nearly all hermits and holy men who live apart from the big cities have the reputation of being able to work miracles with the wild things, but all the miracle lies in keeping still, in never making a hasty movement, and, for a long time, at least, in never looking directly at a visitor. The villagers saw the outline of the barasingh stalking like a shadow through the dark forest behind the shrine; saw the Himalayan pheasant blazing in her best colors before Kali's statue; and the langurs on their haunches, inside, playing with the walnut shells. Some of the children, too, had heard Sona singing to himself, bear-fashion, behind the fallen rocks, and the Bhagat's reputation as miracle-worker stood firm.

Yet nothing was farther from his mind than miracles. He

believed that all things were one big Miracle, and when a man knows that much he knows something to go upon. He knew for a certainty that there was nothing great and nothing little in this world: and day and night he strove to think his way into the heart of things, back to the place whence his soul had come.

So thinking, his untrimmed hair fell down about his shoulders, the stone slab beside the antelope skin was dented into a little hole by the foot of his brass-handled crutch, and the place between the tree trunks, where the begging bowl rested day after day, sunk and wore into a smooth hollow; and each beast knew his exact place at the fire. The fields changed their colors with the seasons; the threshing floors filled and emptied; and again and again, when winter came, the langurs frisked among the branches feathered with light snow, till the mother monkeys brought their sad-eyed babies up from the warmer valleys with the spring. There were few changes in the village. The priest was older, and many of the children who used to come with the begging dish sent their own children now; and when you asked the villagers how long their holy man had lived in Kali's Shrine they answered, "Always."

Then came such summer rains as had not been known in the Hills for many seasons. Through three good months the valley was wrapped in cloud and soaking mist—steady, unrelenting downfall, breaking off into thundershower after thundershower. Kali's Shrine stood above the clouds, for the most part, and there was a whole month in which the Bhagat never caught a glimpse of his village. It was packed away under a white floor of cloud that swayed and shifted and rolled on itself and bulged upward, but never broke from its piers—the streaming flanks of the valley.

All that time he heard nothing but the sound of a million little waters, overhead from the trees, and underfoot along the ground, soaking through the pine needles, and spouting in newly torn muddy channels down the slopes. Then the sun came out, and drew forth the good incense of the deodars and the rhododendrons, and that far-off, clean smell which the Hill-people call "the smell of the snows." The hot sunshine lasted for a week, and then the rains gathered together for their last downpour, and the water fell in sheets that flayed off the skin of the ground and leaped back in mud. Purun Bhagat heaped his fire high that night, for he was sure his brothers would need warmth; but never a beast came to the shrine.

It was in the black heart of the night, the rain drumming like a thousand drums, that he was roused by a plucking at his blanket, and felt the little hand of a langur. "It is better here than in the trees," he said sleepily, loosening a fold of blanket; "take it and be warm." The monkey caught his hand and pulled hard. "Is it food, then?" said Purun Bhagat. As he kneeled to throw fuel on the fire the langur ran to the door of the shrine, crooned and ran back again.

"What is thy trouble, Brother?" said Purun Bhagat, for the langur's eyes were full of things that he could not tell. "Unless one of thy caste be in a trap—and none set traps here—I will not go into that weather. Look, even the barasingh comes for shelter!"

The deer's antlers clashed as he strode into the shrine. He lowered them in Purun Bhagat's direction and stamped uneasily, hissing through his half-shut nostrils.

"Hai! Hai! Hai!" said the Bhagat, snapping his fingers. "Is *this* payment for a night's lodging?" But the deer pushed him toward the door, and as he did so Purun Bhagat heard the sound of something opening with a sigh, and saw two slabs of the floor draw away from each other, while the sticky earth below smacked its lips.

"Now I see," said Purun Bhagat. "The mountain is falling. And yet—why should I go?" His eye fell on the empty begging bowl, and his face changed. "They have given me good food daily since— since I came, and, if I am not swift, tomorrow there will not be one mouth in the valley. Indeed, I must go and warn them below. Back there, Brother! Let me get to the fire."

The barasingh backed unwillingly as Purun Bhagat drove a pine torch deep into the flame, twirling it till it was well lit. "Ah! ye came to warn me," he said, rising. "Better than that we shall do. Out, now, and lend me thy neck, Brother, for I have but two feet."

He clutched the withers of the barasingh with his right hand, held the torch away with his left, and stepped out of the shrine. The rain nearly drowned the flare as the great deer hurried down the slope, sliding on his haunches. When they were clear of the forest more of the Bhagat's brothers joined them. He heard, though he could not see, the langurs pressing about him, and behind them the *uhh! uhh!* of Sona. The rain matted his long white hair into ropes; the water splashed beneath his bare feet, and his yellow robe clung to his frail old body, but he stepped down steadily. He was no longer a holy man, but Sir Purun Dass, K.C.I.E., a man accustomed to command, going out to save life. Down the steep path they poured together, the Bhagat and his brothers, till the deer's feet clicked and stumbled on the wall of a threshing floor, and he snorted because he smelled Man. Now they were at the head of the one crooked village street, and the Bhagat beat with his crutch on the barred windows of the blacksmith's house, as his torch blazed up in the shelter of the eaves. "The hill is falling!" cried Purun Bhagat; and he did not know his own voice, for it was years since he had spoken aloud. "Up and out, oh, you within!"

"It is our Bhagat," said the blacksmith's wife. "He stands among his beasts. Gather the little ones and give the call." It ran from house to house, while the beasts surged and huddled round the Bhagat, and Sona puffed impatiently.

The people hurried into the street—they were no more than seventy souls all told—and in the glare of the torches they saw their Bhagat holding back the terrified barasingh, while the monkeys plucked piteously at his skirts, and Sona sat on his haunches and roared. "Across the valley and up the next hill!" shouted Purun Bhagat. "Leave none behind! We follow!"

Then the people ran as only Hill-folk can run, for they knew that in a landslip you must climb for the highest ground across the valley. They fled, splashing through the little river at the bottom, and panted up the terraced fields on the far side, while the Bhagat and his brethren followed. Up and up the opposite mountain they climbed, and at their heels toiled the big barasingh, weighted by the failing strength of Purun Bhagat. At last the deer stopped in the shadow of a deep pinewood, five hundred feet up the hillside. His instinct told him he would be safe here. Purun Bhagat dropped fainting by his side, for the chill of the rain and that fierce climb were killing him; but first he called to the scattered torches ahead, "Stay and count your numbers"; then, whispering to the deer as he saw the lights gather in a cluster: "Stay with me, Brother.

141

Stay—till—I—go!"

There was a sigh in the air that grew to a mutter, and a mutter that grew to a roar, and the hillside on which the villagers stood was hit in the darkness, and rocked to the blow. Then a note as steady, deep, and true as the deep C of the organ drowned everything for perhaps five minutes, while the very roots of the pines quivered to it. It died away, and the sound of the rain falling on miles of hard ground and grass changed to the muffled drum of water on soft earth. That told its own tale.

Never a villager was bold enough to speak to the Bhagat who had saved their lives. They crouched under the pines and waited till the day. When it came they looked across the valley and saw that what had been forest, and terraced field, and track-threaded grazing ground was one raw, red, fan-shaped smear. That red ran high up the hill of their refuge, damming back the little river, which had begun to spread into a brick-colored lake. Of the village, of the shrine, and the forest behind, there was no trace. For one mile in width and two thousand feet in sheer depth the mountain-side had come away bodily, planed clean from head to heel.

And the villagers, one by one, crept through the wood to pray before their Bhagat. They saw the barasingh standing over him, who fled when they came near, and they heard the langurs wailing in the branches, and Sona moaning up the hill; but their Bhagat was dead, sitting cross-legged, his back against a tree, his crutch under his armpit, and his face turned to the northeast.

The priest said: "Behold a miracle after a miracle, for in this very attitude must all Sannyasis be buried! Therefore where he now is we will build the temple to our holy man."

They built the temple before a year was ended—a little stone-and-earth shrine—and they called the hill the Bhagat's hill, and they worship there with lights and flowers and offerings to this day. But they do not know that the saint of their worship is the late Sir Purun Dass, K.C.I.E., D.C.L., Ph.D., etc., once Prime Minister of the progressive and enlightened State of Mohiniwala, and honorary or corresponding member of more learned and scientific societies than will ever do any good in this world or the next.

Rudyard Kipling
(1865–1936)

BECAUSE KIPLING WROTE so many stories for children, critics once argued that he could never be considered a true literary force. But it was Kipling himself who said, "Give me the first six years of a child's life, and you can have the rest." Perhaps more than any other writer of his age, Kipling understood the importance of writing works that could be appreciated by a broad audience. History has borne him out: Nearly 100 years later, Kipling's poems, *Jungle Book* tales, and novels *Kim* and *Captains Courageous* are considered not only children's classics but some of the finest contributions to English literature.

Kipling was born in Bombay, India, on December 30, 1865, to British artist John Lockwood Kipling and Alice McDonald Kipling, a writer known for her wit and charm. A precocious child, he was encouraged by his parents to develop his creative abilities. Although they often struggled to make ends meet, his parents provided him with a fine upbringing to foster those talents.

For the first seven years of his life, Kipling was placed under the care of an Indian *ayah*, or nurse, and a personal manservant. They opened his eyes to the exotic country in which he lived. His *ayah* taught him Hindi, the local dialect, and took him to places not normally visited by British adults: Hindu temples, Indian private homes, and open markets. These experiences gave him the rare opportunity to observe the differences between the British and Hindu cultures and the conflicts they produced. This knowledge would inform his writing throughout his career.

As was the custom, Kipling was taken to England for his formal education. In 1871, he and his sister Trix were placed under the care of two strangers, Harvey and Rosa Holloway, who lived at a place called the Lorne Lodge on the Devon coast of England. Oddly, the Kipling parents left their children without telling them why they were being separated from the family or whether their parents would someday return for them.

The Kipling children remained with the Holloways for six years, suffering under the cold and spiteful treatment of "Aunty Rosa," as she demanded to be called. Kipling later renamed Lorne Lodge "The House of Desolation" and fictionalized his experience in the harrowing story "Baa, Baa Black Sheep" and in his first novel, *The Light That Failed*.

The Kipling children's only respite from the Holloways came from memories of happier times in India and Christmas holidays, when they visited their mother's sister, Georgiana, and her husband, the painter Edward Burne-Jones. Aunt Georgie and Uncle Ned, as they were lovingly known to the Kipling children, created a magical atmosphere at the holidays, regaling the children with exciting parlor games, magic-lantern shows, and much affection. These vivid memories revealed themselves later, in the colorful imagery of his poems and short stories.

In 1878, Kipling freed himself from Aunty Rosa and began preparatory school at the United Services College at Westward Ho, England. When he graduated, he vowed to become self-supporting by his eighteenth birthday. He also wanted to return to India, the country he loved.

Kipling arrived in India in the fall of 1882 and soon met Stephen Wheeler, a family friend and the editor of the *Civil and Military Gazette* in Lahore. Wheeler hired him immediately as a sub-editor. But Kipling, the precocious child, had become the willful adult and did not fully accept his lowly position. Rather than writing in the rough-and-ready style of the magazine, Kipling submitted articles full of literary flourish. When he refused to change his style, Wheeler consigned him to tedious chores of research and translating from foreign newspaper articles. His only truly important assignment involved covering the summit meeting between the amir of Afghanistan and the governor general of India, Lord Dufferin, in India. The journey provided Kipling with material later translated into *The Jungle Books*.

During this time, Kipling also worked on his short stories and verse, and in 1886, his first poetry collection was published, a book of light verse called *Departmental Ditties*. It was favorably received: the *Times* of India called it "a very pleasant companion for a lonely half-hour or to while away the tedium of a railway journey." Later that year, Stephen Wheeler left the *Gazette* and was replaced by Kay Robinson, who became Kipling's first literary mentor. Robinson sensed that Kipling's talents were "enormously wasted" and created a weekly fiction feature called "Turnovers" to showcase his stories.

In the fall of 1887, Kipling left the *Gazette* and began working for another publication, the *Pioneer,* which had a larger and more cosmopolitan audience. Robinson continued to support Kipling and assembled his best "Turnover" stories in a collection called *Plain Tales from the Hills.* In response to Kipling's growing popularity, the Indian Railway Library also issued seven small collections of his works. These books included some of his most beloved works, including "Wee Willie Winkie."

In 1889, Kipling returned to England to further his writing career. For unknown reasons, he decided to take the long way home, traveling through Hong Kong, Singapore, and the United States. In San Francisco, he made the unpleasant discovery that his reputation as a rising literary light had not preceded him across the Pacific. In fact, his latest works were turned down flat by the San Francisco *Chronicle*, a defeat that may have prompted his unflattering characterization of Americans as people who "talked with an American accent, started getting drunk at 10:30 A.M., and had the vote." Several weeks later, when he reached England, he received a much more cordial reception by its literary figures. By December his verse was published in *Macmillan's Magazine*, and not long after, the Indian Railway series was reissued by a British publishing house and received critical acclaim.

In England, Kipling became friends with Charles Wolcott Balestier, an American publisher who greatly admired Kipling's work. The association was important to Kipling, both professionally and personally. Balestier encouraged Kipling's writing and introduced him to his sister Caroline, with whom Kipling fell in love. While the two men collaborated on a joint fictional venture, the *Naulahka*, Kipling courted Caroline. But the partnership ended tragically when Balestier died of typhoid fever in January 1892. Kipling and Caroline were married in the week following Balestier's death and eventually settled in Caroline's hometown of Brattleboro, Vermont.

Despite Kipling's initial bad impression of America, his stay there was the most productive period of his career. At his country home in the mountains, christened Naulahka in memory of his former collaborator, Kipling wrote his best-remembered works. Among them are *The Jungle Books, Captains Courageous, Barrack Room Ballads*, and the first chapters of *Kim*.

Kipling returned to England in 1896, at the height of his popularity. His success was overshadowed three years later by the death of his daughter, Josephine, who contracted whooping cough during a family visit to the States. Immediately following her death, Kipling returned to England and settled permanently in Sussex. He never revisited the United States. The years to follow brought Kipling's greatest achievements. In 1901, he published *Kim*, the wrenching study of Indian and English relations considered by his critics to be his masterpiece. The following year saw the publication of *Just So Stories for Children*, a now-classic collection for young readers.

All the same, during these years, his critical stature diminished sharply despite the fact that his popularity with general readers remained high. This was due in part to Kipling's facility for children's books, fantasy, and light verse, rather than for more serious literature. Other critics disdained the broad popularity of his works. Still others disagreed with his conservative political views and saw him only as an apologist for the British empire. These opinions persisted, even after Kipling became the first British writer to win the Nobel Prize for literature, in 1907.

Kipling's major efforts in his later years centered on the First World War. When the war broke out in 1914, Kipling immediately became involved with relief efforts, working on behalf of Belgian refugees and with the Red Cross. In 1915, he was a war correspondent, reporting on the French Infantry from the front lines. Three days after his return from France, Kipling was informed that his son, John, was missing in action, though his death was not confirmed until two years later.

Although Kipling never repeated the successes of his early career, he continued to write, focusing on travelogues, political commentary, and war reportage. After a lengthy bout with a duodenal ulcer, Kipling died on January 18, 1936. He is buried in the Poets' Corner of Westminster Abbey.

Other Titles by
Rudyard Kipling

The Beginning of the Armadillos. New York: Harcourt Brace Jovanovich, 1985.

The Best Fiction of Rudyard Kipling. New York: Doubleday, 1989.

Captains Courageous. New York: New American Library, 1980.

Complete Poems: The Definitive Edition. New York: Doubleday, 1989.

The Day's Work. Introduction by Thomas Pinney. New York: Doubleday, 1989.

Gunga Din. New York: Harcourt Brace Jovanovich, 1987.

Just So Stories. New York: Schocken, 1966.

Kim. New York: Dell, 1979.

Life's Handicap: Being Stories of Mine Own People. P. N. Furbank, editor, New York: Penguin, 1987.

The Light That Failed. Introduction by John Lyon. New York: Penguin, 1987.

The Man Who Would Be King & Other Stories. Introduction by Louis L. Cornell. New York: Penguin, 1987.

O Beloved Kids: Rudyard Kipling's Letters to His Children. New York: Harcourt Brace Jovanovich, 1984.

Plain Tales from the Hills. H. R. Woudhuysen, editor. New York: Penguin, 1987.

Puck of Pook's Hill. New York: New American Library, 1988.

The Second Jungle Book. New York: Penguin, 1988.